**'You're certainly a convincing actress, Mel—acting mixed in with a little cunning,' Adam said.**

Melody went to go past him, but he pulled her to him, pinning her arms to her sides, and then his mouth came down on to hers in an angry movement. She felt his tongue probing her lips and she gasped—in surprise and shock at the suddenness of what he was doing. Then...in a moment of unbelievable surrender...she collapsed into his arms. This evening's revelations had been too much for her to cope with—now she needed support. She needed Adam!

Almost at once, the ferocity of his kiss changed into breathtaking passion, and she clung to him. For a few timeless moments they stayed locked together, each lost in their own thoughts, each wallowing in their sudden intimacy...until Melody pulled right away, looking up at him, her eyes glowing with desire—and disillusionment! Because hadn't he just called her deceitful—and *cunning*? Horrible, hurtful words!

**Susanne James** has enjoyed creative writing since childhood, completing her first—sadly unpublished—novel by the age of twelve. She has three grown-up children who were, and are, her pride and joy, and who all live happily in Oxfordshire with their families. She was always happy to put the needs of her family before her ambition to write seriously, although along the way some published articles for magazines and newspapers helped to keep the dream alive!

Susanne's big regret is that her beloved husband is no longer here to share the pleasure of her recent success. She now shares her life with Toffee, her young Cavalier King Charles spaniel, who decides when it's time to get up (early) and when a walk in the park is overdue!

**Recent titles by the same author:**

THE BRITISH BILLIONAIRE AFFAIR
JED HUNTER'S RELUCTANT BRIDE

# THE
# MILLIONAIRE'S
# CHOSEN BRIDE

BY
SUSANNE JAMES

MILLS & BOON

*Pure reading pleasure*™

All the characters in this book have no existence outside the imagination of the author, and have no relation whatsoever to anyone bearing the same name or names. They are not even distantly inspired by any individual known or unknown to the author, and all the incidents are pure invention.

First published in Great Britain 2008
Harlequin Mills & Boon Limited,
Eton House, 18-24 Paradise Road, Richmond, Surrey TW9 1SR

© Susanne James 2008

ISBN: 978 0 263 86479 3

Set in Times Roman 10¼ on 12¼ pt
01-1108-55280

Printed and bound in Spain
by Litografia Rosés, S.A., Barcelona

# THE MILLIONAIRE'S CHOSEN BRIDE

For Toffee,
and my other friends

# CHAPTER ONE

'LADIES and gentlemen—bidding will commence at half past ten exactly. That's in fifteen minutes from now.' The auctioneer's strong, commanding voice cut through the murmuring in the small sitting room and people began to take what seats were available, automatically consulting their own watches and glancing around at the competition.

Melody found a place towards the back, aware that her heart was pounding as she fingered the numbered card in her hand nervously. It stated the number thirty in large black figures and, looking down at it, she still couldn't really believe that she was here, doing this. To call it one of life's amazing coincidences seemed too trite a description. But she *was* here, she was not dreaming, and she was about to take part in the bidding for the rather quaint but very lovely Gatehouse Cottage. And it had certainly not been part of her present holiday plans.

Casting a surreptitious glance around her, she saw that the other interested parties were presumably the kind of eclectic bunch you'd see anywhere, she thought. Ordinary enough people, but today with a single purpose. To buy this property.

Presently there was a hush as the auctioneer took his place at the table, and straight away the atmosphere became charged with expectancy.

'We'll start the bidding at the guide price,' the man said, looking at everyone over his spectacles, 'and I'm going up in tens. Who'll start the bidding for me, please?'

There was an immediate response as someone raised a card, and Melody's breath was almost taken away at the speed with which everything proceeded. Well over the asking price was reached almost at once, before bidding began to slow as bidders shook their heads. Soon it was left to only four hopeful buyers to provide the entertainment. It got slower still as people dropped out one by one, and Melody's mouth was as dry as dust as she continued to raise her card.

Now that she'd started, she just could not stop. For once she was putting her business acumen and expertise into something for *her*—and the experience was a heady one!

Soon there were only two bidders remaining—herself, and a man with a deliciously deep voice at the back of the room, who was just out of her sight. She would actually have had to swivel in her seat to see who was keeping pace with her, so she continued to stare straight ahead.

Swallowing hard, Melody determined to keep on, up to the limit she'd set herself—but equally determined seemed her opponent! But suddenly she was the last bidder, and the all-important gavel was struck sharply once, twice…three times. Gatehouse Cottage was hers!

Melody got up from her place and went towards the desk, where the auctioneer beamed at her. 'Congratulations,' he said kindly.

'Thank you,' she said lightly, by this time feeling in an almost dream-like state. She could barely catch her breath. What had she just done, for heaven's sake?

There was paperwork and official business to see to, and the vital signature to append, but finally Melody left the building and went out into the strong summer sunlight, feeling as important as a middle-eastern tycoon! But she was still shaking inside… She was not usually of an impetuous nature—snap decisions weren't her style—yet she had just entered into an agreement that would now make her the owner of two properties—her apartment in London as well as this idyllic cottage in one of the most beautiful rural spots in England.

Presently, going down the path to reach her car, she almost bumped into someone standing there. A man was leaning nonchalantly against the gatepost, and Melody immediately looked up to apologise—almost swallowing her tongue as she met the searching gaze of the most blue-black eyes she'd ever seen! For a second neither of them spoke, but she was the first to find her voice.

'Oh, I beg your pardon,' she murmured, rather formally, stepping out of his way—but he didn't attempt to move, just stood looking down at her, a faint smile on his lips.

'There's nothing to apologise for,' he said casually, in a darkly rich voice that had the effect of making Melody's spine tingle unexpectedly. 'Except, perhaps,' he added, 'for pipping me at the post just now.' He paused. 'Congratulations, by the way,' he drawled.

So! This was the other determined bidder who'd helped to force the price of the cottage ever higher! He was tall—very tall—and dressed in dark trousers and a shirt which was open at the neck to reveal a tantalising glimpse of black curling hair. Melody looked away quickly.

'Oh—well…' she said, shrugging slightly. 'There must always be winners and losers, mustn't there? But I do hope I haven't ruined your long-term plans too much…'

He raised one dark eyebrow, still staring at her. 'I'll live to fight another day,' he said. He paused. 'But I think the least you can do is to let me buy you some lunch.' He glanced at his watch. 'It's almost midday, and I know a really great pub. I'm hungry after all that tension.'

Melody couldn't help feeling surprised at his suggestion. This man was obviously a fast worker who didn't believe in hanging around—the sort of opportunist that made her feel slightly wary. Then she bit her lip. She'd been too excited—or too nervous—to eat any breakfast at her hotel that morning, and now that she'd secured the deal her appetite was coming back to life!

'All right,' she said, after a moment. 'Why not? 'I'm Mel, by the way.'

'And I'm Adam.' He extended a tanned hand in formal greeting, and grinned in a warm, all-embracing way that had the effect of breaking down any remaining reserve Melody might have felt at accepting an invitation from a complete stranger.

Their cars were parked a little way away along the deserted road. Everyone else had obviously departed. Melody wasn't surprised to see that his was a low-slung, exotic red Porsche. Her own compact Mercedes seemed rather staid by comparison.

'We might as well go in mine,' Adam said briefly, as he flicked the automatic key to unlock his door. 'I can drop you back later.'

'Oh, no, thanks,' Melody said at once. 'I'll follow you to wherever you're taking me. I'll probably want to go on somewhere afterwards, anyway.'

She'd been taught from a very young age not to take anyone at face value, and knew better than to put herself in any kind of vulnerable position. Yet this smooth, suave, unknown male— obviously used to trading on his undoubted good-looks—had coolly invited her out to lunch and she'd agreed straight away! This was not like her, she thought, as she got into her car. But today was a pretty exceptional one, she excused herself. In fact, now that she really thought about it, she knew it was a *fantastic* day! A day to remember, to savour! Enjoy the moment, she told herself. Reality would become apparent all too soon.

Starting the engine and slipping her car into gear, she

followed the Porsche along the blissfully uncluttered roads at a much more respectable pace than she'd imagined they might. He'd seemed the type who'd take pleasure in roaring away in front of her and expect her to keep up with his dizzying assault on the numerous twists and bends they encountered. His whole persona came across as confident, self-assured—a natural leader, accustomed to success and its trappings, Melody thought, and he'd had no problem in getting her to join him for lunch today! But following him on an enjoyable run on this perfect July day had the effect of sending her spirits soaring. If only her mother, Frances, was here now, to share this special morning with her, she thought, her eyes clouding briefly.

In about fifteen minutes they arrived at an insignificant-looking wayside pub, and pulled up simultaneously in the car park at the front. Adam immediately came over and opened her door for her to get out, and Melody was conscious—not for the first time—of how he looked at her, how he was obviously scru-tinising her appearance. She hoped he approved of her white designer trousers and navy and white striped shirt—an outfit she felt was simple but elegantly casual. Her long fair hair she'd tied up in a heavy knot on the top of her head—the style she always used in business. And, after all, today *had* been business—though not the sort that she was usually engaged in. Drawing her hair back formally had the effect of complement-ing the perfect bone structure of her heart-shaped face, her thoughtful grey-green eyes and full-lipped mouth.

Without making any comment, Adam handed her out of the car, and together they walked along the gravelled path to the entrance of the pub. The place was obviously popular, because already it was comfortably full of people. He ushered Melody to a vacant corner table by the window, and looked down at her as she took her seat.

'What are you drinking, Mel?' he asked.

'Just a sparkling water, please,' she said, and he raised his eyebrows slightly.

'No champagne…to celebrate your success today?'

She smiled up at him. 'I'll keep that for some other time,' she said.

She watched him as he went over to stand amongst the jostling crowd at the bar, easily the most noticeable person there. He was taller than anyone else, for a start, she thought, his lithe, athletic body obviously demonstrating a robust and healthy physique. Heavens above, she thought to herself crossly. The day had been enough of an explosive affair as it was…surely she wasn't being blown away by someone she'd probably never see again? Was she that fickle, that pathetic, after losing Crispin not all that long ago? Blame it on today, she excused herself. Today had a definitely weird feel about it!

Presently he came back with their drinks—her water, and a pint of lager for himself—and put a lunch menu in front of her.

'I can recommend the crab cakes,' he said, glancing down at his own copy. 'With the coast so near, the fish is fresh here daily. Or,' he added, looking across at her briefly, 'the barbecued sea bass is also very good.'

By this time Melody's mouth was watering, and she was prompt with her selection. 'I love fish cakes,' she said, 'and I don't often have the chance to eat fresh crab. So crab cakes, please, with a green salad.'

'You're obviously a woman of quick decisions,' he said. 'When I bring people here it usually takes them longer to choose what they want than it does to eat the stuff.'

He got up and went across to order at the bar, glancing back at her as she stared out of the window. This was an unusual woman, he thought. Apart from being very, very, beautiful, she was overtly well dressed, sophisticated, and clearly with a very firm head on her shoulders. The sort of female who knew exactly what she wanted in life and was determined to get it. He'd known many women in his thirty-eight years, but he had the distinct feeling that no one would ever get the better of this one in an argument! She was the kind of woman you wouldn't want to cross, but something about her—especially when he'd observed her at the auction—had excited his curiosity and made him want to find out about her. Who she was…and more importantly why she was taking possession of Gatehouse Cottage.

He returned to sit opposite her. 'So,' he said without preamble, 'you're not from around here, are you?' Well, of course she wasn't…he'd have noticed!

Melody sipped at her water. 'No. I live and work in London,' she said briefly. 'I'm here on holiday for a few weeks.'

Adam frowned. 'But…the auction,' he said slowly. 'How did you know about the cottage being for sale?'

'I was in the village looking around a few days ago and saw the sign. I went into the agent's office and made some enquiries. And…decided to go for it.' She looked up at him calmly, and he stared back at her for a second.

'Do you do that sort of thing often?' he asked. 'I mean, people usually like to buy little mementoes to bring back from a holiday, but a cottage seems rather excessive!'

Melody smiled. 'I agree,' she said. 'And I've never done such a thing in my life before… But…I was attracted to the place… It felt special as soon as I stepped inside. It felt…right, somehow,' she added guardedly.

Adam seemed lost for words suddenly, but her answer only confirmed his opinion of the woman. She knew what she wanted and was going to get it. Whatever the cost. And, talking of cost, she must have the wherewithal to do it, he thought. Not many people had that amount of money instantly at their fingertips!

'Do *you* live locally?' Melody asked, deciding that it was his turn to answer some questions.

'No. I work in Malaysia, where I obviously have to live for most of the time,' Adam said. 'But I always take a long break here, with friends, at about this time every year. Abroad is fine, but rural England is where I feel normal.'

Melody looked away for a second.

'I'm really sorry…to have beaten you at the auction this morning,' she said simply. 'I hope you'll be able to find somewhere else before too long. Not that there seemed much else on offer here… I suppose people just never want to leave the place.'

'You're not sorry at all,' he said cheerfully. 'Besides, someone has to win a battle—as you pointed out—and this time it was you. Maybe there'll be another occasion when I'll have the advantage.'

'Oh, I can't see that happening,' Melody said at once. 'I will not be purchasing another property for a very long time—if ever. A flat in London and a cottage in the country are quite enough for one person to worry about!'

Their meals arrived, and Melody couldn't wait to try the crisp, piping hot crab cakes nestling amongst just the right amount of delicious-looking dressed salad. She picked up her knife and fork and looked across at Adam.

'This all looks yummy!' she exclaimed.

He watched her for a few seconds without starting his own meal. Then, 'What do you intend doing about your living arrangements?' he asked bluntly.

'D'you mean when will I be moving in to the cottage?' Melody asked innocently, between mouthfuls. 'Oh, that's anyone's guess. The previous elderly owner had been there for some years and hadn't done much to the place—so there's obviously some work to do. Everything's still sound enough, but it'll need decorating throughout, and I shall have great fun choosing the right sort of furniture. It's going to be so wonderful to relax here whenever I can get away.' She looked across at him, popping a cherry tomato into her mouth, her eyes shining at the prospect.

'So,' Adam said slowly, 'you've bought the cottage purely as a holiday home? You never intended it to be a permanent dwelling…or maybe a home for your family to share?'

'I don't have any family,' Melody said, rather curtly. 'This is going to be just for me.'

'How often are you likely to be able to get here?' he persisted.

Melody looked away quickly. What right did this man have to interrogate her? she thought. It was none of his business.

'As often as I can,' she said firmly. 'A lot will depend on how things are at work.' She paused, before adding, 'I'm fund manager for one of the big banks,' thinking that she might as well tell him what she did, how she earned her living, before he asked.

He picked up his fork then, and began to eat slowly. Well, what else had he thought? he asked himself. This was clearly a dynamic businesswoman whose daily bread was not likely to be earned in this or any other backwater. 'You won't exactly be number one in the popularity stakes,' he said casually. 'The locals don't take too kindly to absentee property owners… people responsible for killing off villages like these. They want folk to live here and be part of the genuine life of the place— help to keep the school and the post office and the pubs going.'

Melody kept her eyes on her plate, trying not to seethe at the clearly admonishing tone in his remark. Of course she knew exactly what he was talking about. The press regularly ran features about the problem. And she reluctantly had to admit that she hadn't given herself time to really think this through— hadn't got to the point of wondering how often she'd be driving from town, or how long her visits might last. But that didn't stop her thoroughly resenting this stranger giving her a lecture!

'C'est la vie,' she said coolly.

In those few seconds the cordiality of the occasion seemed

to have vanished, and neither spoke for a while as they ate. Then she looked up. 'Let's talk about *you* and your plans,' she said, in a way she recognised as her formal business voice. 'If *you* had succeeded this morning you would obviously have had every intention of living at the cottage permanently, then? Which would have meant abandoning your job in the Far East?'

He returned her gaze, and the eyes which earlier had appeared a friendly blue-black colour now seemed to have acquired a hardened edge. 'Good heavens, no,' he replied casually. 'I can hardly abandon my job—seeing that I'm a partner in the family firm over there.' He finished his meal and put down his knife and fork. 'My father and I transferred the business from England some years ago.'

Well, well, Melody thought cynically. This man, who'd just told her off for helping to 'kill off' the village, thought nothing of taking his family firm out of the country, obviously throwing employees out of work! Talk about double standards! She couldn't let *that* pass!

'So *you* were obviously not "number one in the popularity stakes"?' she said, echoing his own words to her. 'With your ex-staff, I mean. What a miserable bombshell that must have been for them.'

Adam frowned. 'We didn't take the decision lightly,' he said slowly, throwing her a glance which held a hint of disdain at her comments. 'We were able to give them all handsome redundancy payments, and my father—who is very well known in the industry—used his influence to find places for many of the men with our competitors.' He paused. 'He is a very thoughtful man…it caused him a great deal of worry at the time.'

'Mmm,' Melody murmured enigmatically, not wanting to let him off the hook too lightly, yet knowing full well the difficult position companies like his often found themselves in. Her doctorate in Business Studies and Law, together with her masterly understanding of today's commercial world, made it difficult for her not to sympathise.

'So,' she said, as she finished her glass of water, 'if you had managed to secure Gatehouse Cottage this morning, what would *your* plans have been for taking possession?'

'Oh, I didn't have any,' he replied. 'I wasn't bidding for myself. I was there on behalf of friends of mine who have a very special reason for wanting to own it. Friends who've lived in the village all their lives and who have no intention of ever moving away,' he added significantly.

Why was she being made to feel so guilty? Melody asked herself. This morning's business transaction was legal and above board, with the best man winning! It was her good luck—and her considerable financial resources—that had made her the one to buy the cottage, yet the impression she was getting was that she had no right to own the place, and that everyone would hate her for it! This was not the way it was meant to turn out, and being with Adam Whoever-He-Was was making her feel uneasy.

She made a move to go, picking up her bag from the side of the chair.

'Thank you very much for my lunch,' she said, glancing across at him. 'I enjoyed the crab cakes enormously, and I shall come back for some more before I go home.'

He stood up then, tilting his chiselled lips in a half-smile. 'Glad you liked them,' he said. 'Um…wouldn't you like coffee before you go?'

'No, thanks. Not for me,' Melody said. 'I must get back to my hotel—I'm moving out from the Red House today—do you know it? It's very comfortable.'

'Of course I know the Red House. Everyone knows the Red House,' he said off-handedly. 'It's got a formidable reputation in the area. So why are you moving out?'

'I thought I'd come closer to the village. To my new

property,' Melody said neatly, throwing him a glance. 'I rang a B&B that I'd noticed—there are quite a few of them to choose from! Luckily they had a vacancy, so I'll be staying there for a week or two.'

Adam settled the bill at the bar, and they went out into the warm afternoon sunshine. He stood by the side of her car as she opened the door to get in.

'Can you find your way back to the Red House from here?' he asked. 'Or would you like me to lead the way?'

'Oh, there's no need for that—thanks anyway,' Melody said quickly. 'I don't have any problems with route-finding, and I was making mental notes of the direction we were going in as we drove here.' She smiled up at him through the open window. 'And I'm used to reading road signs.'

He shrugged briefly—as if to say, *Well, I was only offering*— then watched her reverse expertly in the confined space of the car park and drive away with a brief wave of her hand as she went.

Adam got into his own car and waited for a moment before switching on the engine. He felt instinctively that this was a rather unusual woman who didn't fit in to his personal categories for the female race. He was certainly attracted to her and, although her petite stature gave her an air of vulnerability, she gave every impression of being someone who was well able to look after herself. Not to mention the fact that she was clearly a very experienced driver who had no difficulty in finding her way around! Now, why should that disturb him in a woman? he asked himself. Most females were rubbish at map-reading, or at even knowing their norths from their souths! But not, apparently, this one!

He stared pensively out of the window for a second. Whether she was brilliant behind the wheel or not wasn't particularly relevant anyway…all he knew was that she was certainly a very intriguing woman—at any rate, she'd intrigued *him* more than anyone had done for a very long time!

He swept out of the car park, smiling briefly to himself, painfully aware that his present, overpowering sensation was one of wanting to cover those dainty, seductive lips with his own! He snorted derisively. Fat chance of *that* ever happening! he thought.

As she made her way back to her hotel, Melody felt such a strange mix of emotions she could have screamed. She should have been thrilled and excited at her purchase that morning, and of course she *was*, yet she realised Adam did have a point about the time she'd be spending at the cottage—actually living there, and buying her bread from the little bakery, fetching her newspaper from the shop. She knew only too well that people like her were a serious irritation who did little to help the local economy.

After she'd driven for a mile or two she pulled in to the side of the road and took the local map which the hotel had given her from her handbag. Although she'd told Adam that she'd have no difficulty finding her way back to the Red House, the fact was she didn't have a clue where she was. But she hadn't wanted to extend her association with the man by accepting his offer that he should shepherd her back. Although he was, without doubt, the dishiest male she'd met in her whole life, she felt that this was not the time to prolong an unlooked-for acquaintance. At this staggeringly unexpected point in her life it would be better to be alone, to think clearly for herself.

The route they'd taken from the village to the pub was unknown to her. All these country roads looked exactly the same as one another, and her hotel was an isolated building that didn't seem to belong anywhere special. Melody sighed as she traced the minute, incomprehensible wiggles on the map with her finger. If the worst came to the worst she could always go right back to the village and set off again from there, she thought. But surely there *must* be a more direct route from where she now was to the Red House?

Feeling that she'd better go back to the pub, she turned the car around and began to drive cautiously along the empty road. Suddenly, rounding a corner, she spotted a woman cyclist ahead of her. Good, she thought. A local who would obviously know where the hotel was.

Pulling up slowly alongside, she opened the passenger window and called out.

'Hello—sorry to bother you, but I'm trying to find my way back to the Red House Hotel. Can you direct me? I'm hopelessly lost!'

The woman—dark-haired and attractive, probably in her mid-thirties, Melody assessed—had an open, friendly expression, and immediately got off her bike—an ancient vehicle with a basket on the front in which were several boxes of eggs. She looked in at Melody.

'I'm afraid you're a bit off-course,' she said, frowning slightly and shielding her eyes from the sun for a second. 'Look, your best bet is to go to the crossroads a mile up the road in front of us, take the left turn, then go on until you come to the smallholding on the right. You can't miss it. There are always two white horses in the field in front. Turn down that road, go on for another mile or so, then the road sort of doubles back on itself before you must take the next right turn. The Red House is there, more or less in front of you. Or should be if *I've* got it right!' the woman said, laughing.

Melody repeated the instructions slowly, hoping she'd find the place before nightfall. The woman's last remark didn't sound particularly convincing! Especially with the added, 'Good Luck!' that she heard as she drove away.

Anyway, she thought, her present confusion would do

nothing to spoil the excitement of the day. Soon, *soon*—when the necessary formalities had been completed—she would be given the keys to her cottage and would be able to revel in really looking around. She would go upstairs and open the door to the little bedroom at the back. The room in which she'd been born.

# CHAPTER TWO

MUCH later in the afternoon, Melody drove up the winding drive that led to the B&B called Poplars, a large Victorian building, and followed the sign to the visitors' car park.

She got out of the car and went towards the large front entrance door. As she entered, a stocky, bearded man came through to greet her, two chocolate Labrador dogs padding behind him. He grinned cheerfully.

'Ah—Mrs Forester? You booked by phone?'

Melody smiled back. 'Yes, that's right.'

He held out a work-roughened hand. 'I'm Callum Brown. I own this place with my wife Fee—or rather, it owns us! I saw you come up the drive, and as you're our last guest due to check in today, I gathered it must be you. Now—shall we fetch your things?'

Together they went across to the car park, the dogs trotting obediently behind Callum. Melody bent to pat them. 'I love dogs,' she said. 'What are they called?'

'Tam and Millie,' Callum said, glancing down at them fondly.

They went back inside, and Melody stood for a few moments at the desk in the hall to sign in.

'Your room is number three, on the second floor,' Callum said. 'I'm afraid we don't run to a lift, so I'll take your cases for you.'

'No need for that, Callum. I'll do the honours. It'll be a pleasure.'

Melody swung around in amazement. She'd recognised the voice straight away, and now found herself staring once more at the man who'd paid for her lunch.

'What…what are *you* doing here? I mean…' she began rather stupidly.

'Staying with friends—as I told you I was,' he replied easily. 'But I didn't realise that Poplars was where you'd transferred to. Anyway,' he added, 'let me make myself useful.' He took her room key from Callum and picked up her cases.

'D'you two know each other, then?' Callum asked curiously.

'Yes, we do. We met at the auction this morning,' Adam said. He paused, then, 'Let me introduce you properly. Mel is the new owner of Gatehouse Cottage, Callum.'

'Well…congratulations,' Callum said slowly. 'You've bought a very desirable property.'

Just then the cyclist whom Melody had spoken to earlier breezed into the hall.

'Oh, *hello* again!' the woman said to Melody, and Melody's heart sank. She hoped that nothing would be said about their afternoon encounter—but no such luck. 'You must be Mrs Forester,' the woman went on. 'The guest who managed to book our last room? I'm *so* glad that you obviously found your way back to the Red House! It was lucky that I was just on my way home after collecting the eggs from the farm.' She turned to the men. 'Mrs Forester got herself *hopelessly* lost this afternoon, trying to get back to her hotel, and she took a surprising risk asking *me* for directions! I'm saying that before either of *you* two do,' she added.

She smiled at Melody, whose face had slowly turned crimson as the woman was speaking. Why did it have to be this particular person she'd asked, a friend of Adam's? What an opportunity for him to gloat, she thought.

'Yes…I did find it, thanks,' she murmured, looking away quickly.

Without saying anything further, Adam led the way along the hall and up two narrow flights of stairs. He glanced back at her over his shoulder. 'I didn't realise you were married,' he said bluntly.

'I'm not,' she retorted.

After that there was silence, then he said casually, 'You'll like it here. Callum and Fee are wonderful people. This place is almost always full—though they always keep a room for me at this time of year.'

'You must be a very special friend,' Melody said flatly.

'Oh, we've all known each other for yonks,' he replied, stopping outside her room and inserting the key.

Melody knew at once that she was going to be happy here. As she'd expected, it was furnished in a cosy way, with a large double bed, comfortable furniture and a very small *en suite* shower room in the corner—obviously a desirable extra which had been recently added on.

'A lot of work's been going on here,' she observed, dropping her handbag onto the bed.

Adam had put down her cases and was standing at the window, looking out. 'They've made a huge difference to the place,' he said. 'Callum does all the renovations himself, and Fee keeps the domestic side going.'

'But she must have help, surely?' Melody said.

'Oh, a girl comes in each morning to help with the breakfasts, and another one arrives later to help with the laundry and cleaning.' He paused. 'And Callum's very hands-on…they're a fantastic team. And still very much in love even after ten years of marriage,' he added, a trifle obliquely.

Melody looked at him quickly, wondering whether he was or ever had been married. There'd been a distinctly cynical ring to his remark, she thought. 'How long have they owned the place, then?' she asked.

'Thirteen years,' Adam said. He turned to look out of the window again. 'They were born in the village, and never want to leave the area.'

The significance of his words wasn't lost on Melody. She was being got at again, she thought irritably. She raised her chin defiantly. It simply was not possible for everyone in the world to live and work in the place of their birth, to stay in one place and do the right thing—much as she acknowledged that the thought of really belonging here, living here all the time, provoked a definite feeling of envy! Her job at the bank was fluid, high-powered and fast moving. At twenty-eight, she was one of the youngest members of staff to hold the position she did, and she was *proud* of her progress—if only for her mother's sake.

She was very well aware how vital it was—especially for a woman—to study and work hard, to dedicate yourself to what you were good at. Success brought not only prosperity, but security and peace of mind. You'd never need to rely on anyone else, ever. No, whatever this man thought of her motives, she thought, there was no way she could ever live here permanently. The only option was for this to be her bolthole as often as she could get away. Gatehouse Cottage was hers, the ideal solution for her particular way of life, and if Adam disapproved—tough! Anyway, wasn't it time for him to make himself scarce and give her some peace to shower and change? she thought.

As if on cue, he went towards the door. 'The couple of pubs in the village do pretty good food,' he said casually. 'Especially the Rose & Crown.' He paused. 'If you'd like me to come with you—as this is your first evening here—I'd be very happy to oblige.'

'Oh—that's okay, thanks,' Melody said quickly. How *embarrassing*! Just because they'd met already, there was no need for him to feel responsible for her, she thought. 'After that lovely lunch I shan't need to eat until later on. In any case,' she added, 'I might go for a walk first, to get an appetite.'

Tilting his head in acknowledgement of her remark, he left the room, and Melody closed the door behind him thankfully. The man's presence unnerved her, she thought—but why? Was it just because she had bought the cottage? Or because he'd made it clear what he thought of holiday ownership? Or was it because he had managed to awaken feelings in her that she was absolutely determined would never affect her life ever again? Her work was her soul mate now, and always would be. Work absorbed the mind totally, and carried no risk of hurting her, of wounding her heart. It was a totally abstract thing that demanded only cold dedication. Work didn't have feelings.

Shaking off all these somewhat intense thoughts, she unpacked her cases, grateful for the huge wardrobe complete with wooden hangers, and then had a long, hot shower, shampooing her hair vigorously. She hoped that by the time she was ready to go back downstairs no one would be about and she could slip out unobserved. She needed to be by herself and take stock of her situation. Perhaps she'd go down to Gatehouse Cottage later and have a really good look at the garden. It had obviously been neglected lately, she realised, but she'd seen the potential at a glance. The gooseberry bushes were heavy with fruit, and the ripening apples and pears on the trees indicated a busy harvesting time later on. Melody hugged herself in renewed excitement.

It was a warm, sultry evening, and she decided to wear a cream, low-necked blouse and a long multi-coloured ethnic cotton skirt. She dried and brushed out her hair, tying it back in a long ponytail, and slipped her feet into open-toed silver sandals.

She went cautiously downstairs. It was quiet and deserted, with a delicious smell of cooking reaching her nostrils—

making her realise that, after all, she was hungry enough to find the pub which Adam had talked about sooner rather than later.

She was just letting herself out of the building when a door in the hallway opened and Fee appeared, her cheeks flushed.

'Oh, there you are, Mrs Forester... We were wondering whether you'd like to have supper with us this evening.' she said 'You'd be more than welcome.'

Melody was taken aback at the suggestion, but managed to say quickly, 'Oh—please call me Mel...all my friends do. And I appreciate the offer, but really I'd hate to intrude. I'm sure you're looking forward to the end of the day and some time to yourself.'

'You wouldn't be intruding,' Fee said. 'Adam's been telling us a little bit about you, and we realise you're a complete stranger here.' She paused. 'Actually, it'd be good to have another woman on the scene to chat to for once, instead of having to listen to Callum and Adam going on and on about boring men things.' She smiled. 'To have a nice gossip! And, since you'll be taking possession of the cottage, we could fill you in on how everything ticks in the village. I've roasted a wonderful piece of lamb,' she added. 'Because if I dish up one more salad meal I'll have a mutiny on my hands! What's the matter with men and salad?' she said.

She nodded her head in the direction from which male voices could be heard, and Melody found herself unable to resist the genuine invitation she'd been offered.

'Well—if you're absolutely sure,' she began hesitantly.

'Wonderful!' Fee said. 'Come on through. It'll be ready in about twenty minutes. Just time for an appetiser!'

Although she'd really have preferred to do her own thing tonight—mainly because she didn't particularly want to spend more time in Adam's company—Melody knew it would have been churlish to refuse Fee's suggestion. Besides, the smell of roasting meat was extremely tantalising!

She followed the other woman along a narrow passageway that led to the kitchen, where Adam was already sitting comfortably with his long legs stretched out in front of him, while Callum was busy uncorking a bottle of wine. Both men looked up as they came in, and Adam got slowly to his feet.

'Ah, good,' Callum said easily. 'I want your opinion on this wine, Mrs Forester. I bottled it two years ago, and we haven't tried it yet.'

'Look—*please* call me Mel,' Melody begged. 'Do you make your own wine, as well as everything else you do?' she added, impressed. She bent to smooth the glossy heads of the dogs, who were fast asleep sprawled in front of the Aga.

Callum grinned. 'Oh, my wife beats me about the head if she finds me shirking,' he said. 'And we can't let all the plums and damsons go to waste.' He eased the cork out gently. 'Besides, what we don't keep for ourselves we sell off at the village fête. It disappears even quicker than Fee's fruitcakes!' He threw her a quizzical glance. 'I don't expect you're used to the sort of daft things we get up to,' he said. 'Like pig roasts and skittle championships, and tugs of war at the annual Harvest Fair. Not your usual scene, from what Adam has been telling us. Still, I'm sure you'll get used to it, in your own time.'

Melody looked away. What exactly had Adam been saying about her? she wondered. That she was never likely to fit in here, never be 'one of them'? She began to feel uneasy.

Adam pulled out a chair for her to sit, glancing down at her, admiring her casual, summery appearance, and the feminine hairstyle which seemed to add something to the package, he thought. Or maybe it took something away—whatever it was, it held more allure for him than the rather sharp-edged look he'd observed that morning.

Callum took a sip of his wine. 'Mmm,' he said, rolling his tongue around his mouth in extravagant appreciation. 'I think you're all going to approve of this. How shall we describe it? Fruity, nutty, saucy, suggestive…?'

'Shut up, Callum,' Fee said. 'Give us all a glass, for goodness' sake. Why do we have to go through this ridiculous rigmarole every time you open a fresh bottle? Just let's drink it, then can you come and carve the meat, please?'

Melody took a few tentative sips of the wine and realised that it was the most delicious she'd tasted in a long time. 'This is fantastic, Callum! It beats champagne by a mile,' she added, taking another generous mouthful.

'Oh, I'm afraid we don't have much experience of drinking champagne,' Callum said easily. 'Though I think we had sparkling wine at our wedding, didn't we, Fee?'

Melody bit her lip, feeling her colour rise. She hadn't meant to give the impression that she was a connoisseur—though it was certainly true that she was offered plenty of expensive wines in her career. What sort of impression was she giving these people? Especially after her extravagant purchase that morning, she thought desperately.

The episode passed as Callum got to work with the carving knife, while Fee put bowls of vegetables and a large plate of crisp brown roast potatoes in front of them. Adam sat down next to Melody, and conversation paused significantly while they all helped themselves to the mouthwatering food. And although Melody felt uneasy, and somewhat out of place sitting here with these complete strangers, she couldn't help enjoying the feeling of being made welcome. And it wasn't long before the wine kicked in, making her feel warm, tingly and relaxed.

It was nearly ten o'clock before she decided to call it a day, and she realised how good it had felt to be with people who were not involved with work. Even though the staff often called in at a wine bar on the way home, or had the occasional meal together, it was always a case of talking shop. This had been different.

After thanking her hosts profusely, she stood for a moment outside, breathing in the soft evening air, and as it was still not quite dark she decided to go for a short stroll. This was the sort of thing you could do in a quiet retreat like this, she thought, as she walked noiselessly down the drive—there was no sense of danger lurking around every corner, no dark-hooded yobs hanging about, and the only sounds were the occasional baaing of a sheep or the hoot of a night owl.

She wandered along the few hundred yards towards Gatehouse Cottage. Not that she would be actually given the keys until the day after tomorrow, when all the financial arrangements had been completed—but it would be good to just stand in her very own front garden and plan the future. And not only that, she realised. The future was one consideration, but she also wanted to visit the past—a past which she had not seen fit to talk about to the others. It was not important to anyone but her, after all.

It took only three or four minutes to get to the cottage, and she paused before silently opening the small wooden gate and going up the path.

She peeped in through one of the windows—which was in need of a good scrub, she noticed—and stared in at the sitting room. She couldn't see much in this light, but, cupping her hands around her eyes, she could just make out its shape, and the open grate in the corner. She'd have a log fire there one day, she promised herself. On a grey morning that room would spring to flaming life.

Suddenly something wet touched her ankle, followed by a snuffling sound, and Melody jumped, letting out a faint cry of alarm. She sprang back and turned quickly to see one of the Labradors gazing back at her solemnly. Then Adam's voice sounded through the darkness.

'I knew I'd find you here,' he said quietly. He paused. 'I volunteered to give the dogs their nightly stroll,' he went on. 'Tam didn't frighten you, did he?'

'No, of course not!' Melody lied. She swallowed nervously. 'My instinctive thought was that it might have been a fox…or a badger…'

'Well, would that have worried you?' he asked casually.

'No…it was just…I didn't expect to have company—of any sort,' she said.

Melody's instinctive sense of irritation at being followed had been replaced almost at once by one of mild relief at not being down here alone, and she bent quickly to pat the animals. Although she'd convinced herself that this quiet rural paradise was her dream, in fact she felt slightly wary at just how solitary it was. The silence was deafening, and with no street lights at this point the darkness was very dark indeed. She'd already made a mental note to have a security light put over the front door.

After a moment, she said casually, 'I didn't think I'd be able to get to sleep very easily—especially after that rhubarb crumble and clotted cream,' she added, as she came to stand next to him. 'So I thought a walk seemed sensible.'

'Well, you haven't had much of one,' he said. 'From Poplars to here, I mean.' He paused. 'I could take you for a slightly longer one, if you like…' He glanced down at her feet. 'Will you be able to walk in those sandals?'

'Of course I can. As long as we aren't going to cross a river.'

'No rivers,' he replied shortly. 'Just half a meadow and a couple of small copses. It's a favourite track behind Poplars and back again. The dogs will lead the way.'

They fell into step, and Melody was struck again at how this was such a long way from her flat in a busy street where the sound of traffic never stopped. She looked up at Adam. 'I really can't believe my luck,' she said simply. 'Although if you'd bid one more time I'd have stopped.'

He waited before answering. 'Do you mean that? Was I that close?'

'Oh, yes,' Melody said at once. 'It was touch and go—but you stopped at just the right moment!' There was a short silence, then, 'Anyway,' she went on happily, 'you said you didn't want the cottage for yourself, didn't you? After you'd told me that I didn't feel so bad about it! But I hope the friend who was interested will find something else soon.'

'Oh, it's too late now,' Adam said briefly.

He glanced down at her, and by now Melody had grown accustomed to the light, so she could make out his features and rather dark expression. 'Too late? What do you mean?'

He waited before going on. 'I was bidding for Callum and Fee,' he said. 'They really wanted to have the cottage—it's been their ambition for years. Poplars and the Gatehouse were originally linked—as you'll have noted from the agent's blurb—and it was their aim to own both so that one day, when they retire, the cottage would be their family home. The hard-earned profit they've made on the guesthouse allowed them to go for it.'

Melody swallowed. Now she felt worse than ever! She'd unwittingly thwarted the plans of that lovely local couple…and not a word had been said about it during the meal. Well, what was there to say? she thought. What could they have said? They'd lost the chance, and business was a chancy thing—everyone knew that.

'But…but…they wouldn't have lived in the cottage, would they? Not while they were running Poplars?' Melody said, trying to quell her feelings of disquiet.

'No. Not yet. But in the meantime they intended renting it on a long-term lease to any local couple who needed a place to live. We're so desperately short of affordable housing for the younger generation and they're all moving away. In another ten or fifteen years the village will just be full of older people and tourists. And part-time owners like yourself.'

For once, Melody felt lost for words. She could see the point he was making—in no uncertain terms! But she could see her own, too. It had seemed so right that the place was for sale at the very time she was in the area on holiday. Was fate trying to tell her something, giving her the chance to find out what she'd always wanted to know? A chance to unwrap something of herself that had lain hidden for so long?

Neither spoke for the next few moments as they trod easily over the soft, dry grass of the meadow. Then Melody said, 'I'm amazed that I was invited to share that fantastic meal...to be their guest. They must hate me—or at least bitterly resent me,' she added.

'Oh, Callum and Fee aren't like that,' Adam said at once. 'They don't bear grudges.' He shrugged. 'They knew all along that it was more than probable that someone else would beat them. They've accepted it gracefully.'

He didn't look at her as he spoke, nor mention the fact that it had been his suggestion that she should be included in their supper arrangements. For one thing, he'd thought it would be useful to have some idea what this woman's plans were for when she came to the village, and for another—and a more pressing one—he wanted to know what she was *really* like. He readily admitted that she fascinated him, and not only because of her outward appearance. There was something about her, some inner thing that intrigued him. And if he wanted to get to know her, there was no time like the present!

'Callum and Fee...they don't have children?' she asked— and the question made Melody think briefly of her own life plan. She and Crispin had met at work, and both had been equally ambitious. She'd had vague notions of motherhood, maybe in ten years' time, but their careers had always taken first place. A family had definitely been a back burner issue.

'No,' Adam replied shortly, in answer to her question. 'They don't.'

They walked on slowly, neither wanting the evening to end, because it was one of those rare warm summer nights with hardly any breeze, and a pale moon to give them just enough light to see their way.

'This is so heavenly,' Melody murmured. 'Like a dream.'

'What happened to your marriage?' Adam said suddenly, without the slightest embarrassment at asking the question.

'My husband—Crispin—was killed in a climbing accident last year in the Himalayas,' Melody said quietly.

Adam looked at her sharply. 'Oh—I'm sorry—really. I shouldn't have asked,' he said.

'We'd been married for just a few months.'

'That was bad. I'm sorry,' he repeated.

She looked so small and defenceless as he glanced down at her that for a mad moment he wanted to pull her towards him and hold her tightly. But he resisted the temptation.

'And you?' she enquired. 'You're not married?'

'No, thanks,' he said cheerfully.

Well, Melody thought, that was a fairly unequivocal reply! Anyway, something about this man told her he wasn't the marrying kind. He'd be the sort who enjoyed women's company for the obvious reason, but would never be happy to settle down, commit to one person. She frowned to herself, not knowing what had given her that impression. But something about his attitude made her think that he was of a restless nature.

Suddenly she said, 'I did get lost this afternoon—trying to find my way to the Red House—as Fee informed everyone.'

He smiled faintly in the darkness. 'We all get lost sometimes,' he said.

'You knew I'd have difficulty, didn't you?'

'Yes. Especially as you roared off in the wrong direction,'

he replied. 'But I knew you'd succeed eventually. And everyone speaks English here!'

Their walk came to an end, and they let themselves in quietly.

'For your future reference,' Adam said softly, 'they lock up at midnight.'

'I'll remember,' Melody said. She turned to go towards the stairs. 'Thanks for the stroll, Adam. I'm sure I'll be repeating that many times.'

'I'm sure you will,' he murmured. Then, 'D'you think you can find your way to your room?' he enquired innocently.

Melody smiled ruefully. 'I deserved that,' she said. 'Goodnight.'

'Goodnight, Mel.'

Melody undressed quickly, washing and cleaning her teeth rapidly, before pulling back the duvet and collapsing into the feather-soft bed. It was heaven to lie down, and she was exhausted. What a day! Her head was so packed with thoughts and emotions that it felt as if thousands of insects were racing around, trying to find space. Almost at once her eyelids began to droop, and in her semi-doze Adam's handsome features, with the stern, uncompromising mouth, loomed large. She didn't know what to make of him, she thought. He didn't like *her* much; she was certain of that. Although he was perfectly polite—even charming at certain moments—there was a coolness between them which she'd felt from the first moment.

Of course he was cross that she'd upset his friends' plans…but what about *her* plans? This village was where she'd started life, and Poplars had been her mother Frances's sole means of employment until she'd had Melody at the age of forty, when she'd promptly moved with her newborn child to the east end of London to live with a cousin. Melody had been twenty-two, in the middle of her Finals at university, when

Frances had died suddenly. And in all those years Frances had never revealed who the father of her child was—had been so secretive about that part of her life that discussion on the matter had become almost a taboo subject. All she would ever tell her daughter was that she had loved deeply, only the once, and that certain things could not be spoken of, that some words were better left unsaid.

Melody had had to be content with that. But somewhere in this village there was a living part of her, part of her mother and the father she would never know, and somehow she knew that just by being here, breathing this air, she was completing her family circle so that she almost felt as if she was being embraced. So didn't *she*, Melody, have her own very personal reasons for wanting to live here again, even on a part-time basis? Wasn't she entitled to return to the family nest, to the village where her mother, too, had been born? How much more right did anyone need to belong here?

She turned over, flinging her arm across the pillow.

She opened her eyes and stared around the room for a moment. Her mother must have cleaned this place hundreds of times when she was housekeeper here, she thought. Servicing all these rooms and cooking for the Carlisle family, who'd owned Poplars for three generations, must have been desperately hard work. Melody's eyes misted for a moment, thinking of Frances's determination that her daughter should be qualified and independent. That education was the way up and the way out. So whatever life threw at her, her girl would always be able to stand on her own feet and follow her dreams. And that was what she was doing now!

In his own room on the ground floor, Adam slumped in an armchair by the window, feeling wide awake and knowing that he wasn't likely to get to sleep easily. He knew he was still upset at letting the cottage slip through his fingers—and especially upset to lose it to a woman—a stranger to the village—who'd bought the place on a whim.

He clicked his tongue in annoyance at the thought that if he'd bid just once more he'd have won. But he'd already exceeded the stake he'd put in of his own money, to help his friends out, and hadn't wanted to undermine Callum's confidence by upping and upping the price unreasonably. Callum was such a straightforward, honest man, and he and Fee had already repaid every penny that Adam had lent them way back, when they'd first purchased Poplars. They'd worked so incredibly hard to be able to do that. Now this woman had sauntered in and stolen the cottage from under their noses.

After a few moments, his mind took another turn. He had to admit that Mel seemed much nicer than she'd appeared at first...not so damned sure of herself. His lip curled faintly. She'd jumped nearly a foot into the air when Tam had licked her leg, and he'd sensed her edginess a mile off! He paused in his thoughts. It must have been a terrible blow to be widowed so soon after her marriage—though she obviously had no financial worries, he mused. His eyes narrowed briefly. Maybe all was not lost, after all...

Was it just possible that he might be able to change the course of things, make her change her mind and sell it to his friends after all? It was a long shot—he knew that—but it was worth a try. Another place would come up sooner or later, if buying a country retreat was really what she wanted. He stood up restlessly. She was going to be here for a few weeks yet, so she'd said. That should be long enough for him, Adam Carlisle, to demonstrate his masculine powers of persuasion. But he'd have to be clever about it. This woman was worldly-wise, unlikely to be a push-over, in any circumstances—and she was intelligent and perceptive. She'd spot his motives a mile off if he went blundering in. No—softly, softly, with a dose of gentle cunning, *might* work. He unbuttoned his shirt, shrugging it off. Something told him he was going to enjoy this!

## CHAPTER THREE

Two days later Melody stood once more outside her cottage, this time with a set of keys in her hand. Everything had been signed, sealed and delivered, and now the only person who had a legal right to enter the place was her! Melody Forester!

She waited a moment before opening the door, realising for the first time just what lay ahead of her. Before she was due to return to London in a couple of weeks there was a lot of work to be done! But she'd get things moving straight away, she thought decisively. First of all she'd hire someone to help her clean the place right through, and then she'd go shopping for curtains and floor coverings. The cottage was absolutely devoid of anything, except some ancient lino in the kitchen, so at least she had a clean sheet and could start from scratch. Of course she couldn't do everything at once, but she'd make a jolly good start, and then focus her mind on the kind of furniture she wanted. It would be simple, but comfortable.

She smiled to herself. She was supposed to be here on holiday, to rest and recharge her batteries after the heavy but very successful year which her team had had—and here she was, giving herself another set of problems with decisions to be made. Holiday? What holiday!

She unlocked the front door and stepped into a small hallway which led almost at once into the sitting room—which had windows at either end, making it light and airy. She stood quite still for a moment. In a strange way she almost expected her mother to appear, for this had been Frances's home for more than twenty years—all the time she'd been employed at Poplars—and in spite of the total nakedness of the place, the atmosphere felt warm and welcoming to Melody. She felt oddly connected here. It felt like home, and that was what she would make it. Even if Adam Wotsisname didn't approve, she'd come here time and time again—make it a home from home!

She bit her lip thoughtfully. She hadn't seen Adam since that first evening—for which she was thankful. She didn't want any hindrances, any bothersome ties here, and something about him suggested that he could be somewhat over-helpful if she gave him the slightest encouragement. Then she felt guilty— what had he done except buy her lunch and take her for a moonlit walk? In his way, he was sort of charming—and annoyingly handsome, it had to be admitted—but his attitude had rankled from the start. He patently considered her an outsider, and had no problem declaring the fact.

There was only one other room downstairs. It was small, but would be useful as a study if she needed one—or it could even be used as an occasional third bedroom. She didn't doubt that she'd have plenty of takers among her colleagues for the chance of a short holiday here now and then!

With her feet echoing on the wooden floors, she went up the narrow stairway and into the back bedroom where, apparently, she'd first seen the light of day. From its window she not only had a full view of her garden, but in the near distance over the tops of the trees she could just see the roof of Poplars. She stood quite still for a moment, a frown crossing her features. Why *was* it that her mother had never wanted to come back to the area—even for a short visit?

Melody had been told so much about the way of life in the village—the wonderful walks and peaceful atmosphere which Frances had loved—yet her mother had always made some excuse or other not to return. No—it had been beyond excuses. It had been a firm decision that that part of her life was over. For ever.

Melody shrugged, kneeling forward on the shabby cushioned window seat as she continued to gaze at the scene below. Suddenly there was a light tap on her front door, and Adam's voice calling from below halted her in her reverie. She tutted to herself—he hadn't wasted any time, she thought. She'd only taken possession of the cottage half an hour ago!

She heard him run swiftly up the stairs, his strong footsteps echoing through the place, and he came straight in to stand next to her. She turned to look up at him, trying to look pleased at his unexpected entrance. He was wearing jeans and a fine grey T-shirt, and his dark hair shone with healthy vigour...though he did tend to wear it rather long. Not that it didn't suit his persona, she admitted—it was just that the men she usually mixed with all seemed to favour neat and formal hairstyles.

He was holding a huge bouquet of roses and lilies, and he thrust them forward. 'Morning, Mel,' he said easily, smiling down at her. 'Just a small welcome gift for your first day.'

Melody was genuinely touched. 'Oh...how lovely! And how unexpected!' She took the bouquet from him, examining it appreciatively. 'You must have known that these are my all-time favourites! But—*thank* you...you shouldn't have!'

'Oh, I think I should,' he said, going over to the window, his hands in his pockets. 'Buying houses isn't an everyday occurrence, is it? At least, not for most people,' he added. 'I've brought a vase down from Poplars, by the way.'

'Yes...I've just been thinking about all the stuff I'm going to have to buy,' Melody said. 'I hadn't got around to the question of vases yet! But I shall certainly need some, because flowers always light up a house, don't they?'

He glanced down at her, thinking how exquisite she looked in a fresh, simple green cotton sundress which showed off the lightly tanned, smooth skin of her neck and shoulders to perfection. Her long pale hair was pulled back casually and held with a tortoiseshell clip. He'd noticed at their first meeting that she wore very little make-up, but what she did use certainly suited her, because from her appearance she might have stepped from the pages of a glossy magazine. This place didn't need flowers to light it up, he thought. She did that all by herself!

He pulled his thoughts up sharply. He didn't want to admire this woman to the point where he started to feel anything for her, he told himself. If it hadn't been for her, the cottage's ownership would have been in very different hands, and it still peeved him beyond words that he hadn't gone the extra mile. But how *could* he have known that he was so close? He'd only seen her, the other bidder, from the back during the auction, but there'd been something about the way she'd sat there that morning—the angle of her head, the slim, determined hand that had kept raising her card—depicting a businesswoman who was used to getting what she wanted.

He turned away briefly. What was done was done—for the moment. He knew it was a long shot, but he did have a little time to perhaps change things, to make her see just what she had taken on and maybe convince her that this wasn't what she really wanted. That it could become more of a burden than a bonus if it turned out that she simply did not have enough time away from her London life and job to justify the financial outlay and upkeep. He also felt instinctively that a town was where she fitted in—where everything you needed was on tap at all hours of the day. In this village tomorrow was always deemed soon enough for most people!

Allowing her to go first, they went downstairs, and Melody turned on the kitchen tap and filled the large glass jug which Adam had brought with him. Pausing for a moment, she said lightly, 'I really don't know where to start. I mean…this kitchen could do with some work, though it seems to have been refitted at some point in the past.' She looked around her doubtfully, then opened the fridge door and peered inside. 'This is clean enough—and I suppose I won't need anything any bigger.' She stood back. 'But there's no washing machine, and I'll certainly need one of those…'

'The last owner died,' Adam said matter-of-factly. 'That's why the place came on the market. And I think the washing machine was in a bad way, so it was chucked.'

'I wonder if there's room for a dishwasher—' Melody began, and he interrupted.

'Oh, I don't think this kitchen has ever sported one of those. I'm afraid you'll have to do everything by hand, Mel!'

Melody said nothing as they wandered into the sitting room, where the sun was streaming in through the windows, lighting up all the dusty corners.

'What are those two boxes on the floor doing there?' Melody said, frowning.

'Oh, I brought them with me—for us to sit down on,' Adam said, promptly kicking one to one side and taking up position. 'It's quite comfy, actually—who needs expensive chairs? Now, then—' he rubbed his hands together briskly '—I've come to help!'

Melody looked at him, a faint feeling of hopelessness sweeping over her. This man was here to stay! Her worst fears were being realised! She was not going to be allowed to be anonymous, to be by herself and work things out quietly and in her own time.

She placed the flowers carefully on the windowsill, and turned to look down at him.

'I really don't want to take up your time, Adam, or for you to use up your holiday on my behalf,' she said evenly. 'I'm sure you've other far more interesting things to think about than me and my cottage.'

'Oh, not true,' he said at once. 'As a matter of fact, I've already been here a number of weeks, and I was beginning to get quite bored. Your current project might prove to be an interesting diversion for me—and, well, you know, a pair of brawny arms can be useful at times.'

He looked pointedly at her own slender frame in a way which made Melody's colour rise, and she shrugged resignedly. The fact was that being here now, in the revealing light of day, had made her feel less sure of herself. When they'd bought and furnished their flat in London, Crispin had been there, and they'd worked as a team and had lots of interested friends all helping out. But now she was here, alone, in virtually unknown territory—even though her mother had spoken many thousands of words about the place, which had made it *seem* familiar.

Melody's earlier euphoria was threatening to give way to a feeling of doubt. Had purchasing the cottage been something that she was going to regret? she wondered. Then she scolded herself! What was the matter with her? This wasn't like her. Of *course* she'd cope alone—hadn't her mother had to do that, all her life?

'I vote that we first of all go to the Rose & Crown for coffee,' Adam said brightly, 'and then decide on a plan of action.'

'It can't be that time already, surely?' Melody said, glancing at her watch. 'Anyway, Fee's breakfasts are so generous, coffee will seem an unnecessary indulgence.'

She couldn't remember the last time she'd enjoyed lazily eating bacon, eggs, sausages and mushrooms, followed by lovely warm, crunchy toast and fresh farmhouse butter. Not to mention home-made marmalade!

'Well, holidays are a time for indulging ourselves,' Adam said firmly.

Melody looked at him shrewdly. There was a distinct change in his attitude from when they'd first met, she thought—the animosity he'd demonstrated seemed to have disappeared. Her eyes narrowed briefly. If he thought that he'd met someone who'd be good for a holiday fling, he was going to be disappointed. She was not on the market for such things, thanks very much.

Patting the other box for her to sit down, Adam leaned back nonchalantly. 'See—this feels cosy already,' he said, his eyes twinkling mischievously.

'Um, well…not as cosy as it *will* do—in time,' Melody retorted as she sat down as well.

'Talking of which,' he went on, 'how much time *do* you have?'

'Just under two weeks—' she began, and he cut in.

'Your employers are very generous,' he said. 'From what you've told me, you'll have had about six weeks off, won't you? Do *all* the staff enjoy such annual freedom?'

'Some do—sometimes,' she replied shortly. 'We've had an exceptionally tough time this last year. We—me and the rest of the team—often don't leave the office until ten o'clock or after, and we always start early. They are very long days,' she added, trying to hide the irritation she felt at having to defend herself. What did *he* know?

'Mmm… You're a fund manager, you said?' he went on. 'It must be fun, playing around with other people's money.' He'd only made the remark to annoy her. He realised only too well what a highly skilled and specialised job it was.

'Oh, it's great fun. A real laugh,' Melody said dryly. 'We all sit there, playing Monopoly with millions and millions of pounds which don't belong to us.' She paused. 'For your information, we spend hundreds of hours researching the companies we invest in on behalf of others, going over and over it until we're satisfied. Being in charge of pension schemes, where we're fully aware how we affect people's future well-being, is a nail-biting process which is taken very seriously.' Her eyes flashed as she spoke, as she relived just how much effort everyone had put in during the year to keep pace with the country's fluctuating economy and prospects.

After a few moments she calmed down. He'd made a flippant remark which she'd taken too seriously, she reasoned. She had the distinct impression that he'd only said it to get her going—and she'd taken the bait!

Adam had been watching her closely as she'd been speaking. 'Do you like what you do? Do you enjoy it?' he asked casually.

'Yes, of course! I wouldn't do it otherwise. I can't see myself doing anything else, ever.'

Well, he'd known she was a career woman. She was not going to tear herself away and come all the way down here just for a few days now and then. It was a total waste for her to own this cottage, he thought. It was like a spoilt child, seeing something in a shop window that he thought he wanted but which would never leave the toy cupboard.

'Anyway,' she said, 'I don't want to think about work—there are other things on my mind! I need to hire someone to clean the cottage from top to bottom. I expect there are locals who might be glad of some work?'

'Oh, don't count on that,' he said bluntly. 'Casual labour isn't that easy to come by—just ask Fee! All the guesthouses use up most of what's on offer.' He paused. 'And I'm afraid we don't run to agencies here, to cope with such demands.' He grinned. 'I'd hazard a guess that it's going to be just you and me, Mel!' Looking at her soft hands and beautifully manicured nails, he smiled inwardly. She might be a whiz-kid at what she did for a living, but he somehow couldn't imagine the woman down on her knees with a scrubbing brush!

Melody shrugged. 'Well, in that case the first thing will be to buy cleaning materials,' she said, fielding his remark briskly. She knew very well what he was thinking: that she wasn't used to domestic labour. Well, he'd got another thing wrong, she thought. Even though her mother had always put education at the top of the list for her daughter, Frances had also encouraged Melody to help with everything in the house—and she had. And when Frances had been unwell, which had been the case often in the years before the woman's untimely death six years ago, Melody had taken over. Shopping, cooking a nourishing meal and baking a cake were no problem!

'And what about you and *your* extended holiday?' Melody asked suddenly. 'I suppose being the privileged son in a family business means you have all the perks—which obviously means lots of time off. I wonder what the other staff think of that!'

'Oh, the staff don't have any problems with that,' he said, unperturbed at her remarks. 'In fact, they are extremely happy with their lot. They've never had it so good, and they're grateful.'

Suddenly a light footstep outside heralded Fee's appearance, and she popped her head in through the open door, beaming at Melody.

'I just had to call by and say welcome to our new neighbour,' she said, and Melody was struck by Fee's kind enthusiasm—which was more than generous in view of the circumstances.

She came in and looked around her, and Adam immediately stood up.

'Come and sit down on this lovely upholstered seat, Fee,' he said jovially. 'Not quite up to modern standards, but needs must.' He pulled the woman gently towards him on to the box he'd been sitting on, and just then his mobile rang. He wandered outside to answer it. Fee looked across at Melody.

'You must be thrilled, Mel,' she said simply. 'This is going to be such a lovely change from your home in London.'

'Yes, of course…' Melody replied quickly, feeling slightly awkward. 'You run a marvellous guesthouse, Fee,' she said hurriedly. 'Everything seems to run like clockwork. Which means, of course, that someone—you—works extremely hard all the time. Success at anything never happens by chance, does it? It's always hard graft in the end.'

Fee sighed, wiping her forehead with a tissue, and closing her eyes briefly. 'I'm used to hard work.'

Melody looked at her quickly. 'Are you all right, Fee?' she said. 'You do look rather warm…'

'Oh, yes—I'm fine,' Fee said, smiling briefly. 'As a matter of fact… Oh…it doesn't matter…'

'Go on,' Melody said gently, sensing that the woman wanted to talk.

Fee waited a moment before going on. 'It's just that I'm pregnant, Mel—after all this time, after all the false alarms and disappointments.'

'But that's terrific—fantastic, Fee!' Melody said enthusiastically. She had no doubt that Callum and Fee would make the most wonderful parents.

'We've not told anyone yet—not even Adam,' Fee said, lowering her voice, and Melody thought Adam must be a very special friend if he was usually privy to all their important news. 'He's known all about my past problems,' Fee went on, 'but it's a bit soon, and I don't want anyone to get excited on our behalf. Not until I've passed the three-month stage—which isn't quite yet.'

'Well—thank you for letting *me* into the secret,' Melody said warmly. 'And I won't breathe a word!' She paused. 'But shouldn't you be taking it easy—you know, with your feet up?'

Fee smiled. 'That'll be the day, Mel,' she said. 'If this time it's meant to be, putting my feet up or not won't make any difference—though of course if it proves to be the real thing I'll be taking full advantage of the situation! I'll have everyone running around after me, obeying orders…'

Both women laughed at the unlikely thought of Fee remaining idle for long, and Melody said, 'Adam seems very…I mean, you've known each other for a very long time, obviously…'

'Oh, yes. He and Callum started school together. They're both thirty-eight now. And then of course Adam and his twin brother Rupert went to boarding school at the age of nine, then on to university—they never really came back here to live much at all.'

'Oh…I didn't know Adam had a twin brother,' Mel said, surprised at herself for *being* surprised.

'No—that's seldom mentioned,' Fee said quietly. 'There's a bit of bad blood there, I'm afraid…'

Melody couldn't help feeling curious at this last bit of information, but didn't pursue the matter.

'Then, of course, their parents decided to sell Poplars, and—'

Melody was mystified. 'D'you mean that *they*—Adam's family—owned the place? Owned Poplars?'

'Oh, yes. Didn't you realise? The Carlisle family owned Poplars and the Gatehouse for three generations, but about fifteen years ago Isabel and Robert—Adam's parents—decided to sell up because they were away such a lot. They're great travellers—quite apart from the time they have to spend in Malaysia—and they thought it was a shame for the place to be empty for such long stretches. So they sold the two properties to a local couple—both vets—but their marriage fell apart almost at once, and everything came up for sale again. That was when we just managed to afford Poplars. The cottage was bought by a man from the next village. He died at the end of last year—and, well, the rest you know.'

For a few minutes Melody was stunned into silence. No wonder Adam had such tight-lipped ideas about the two properties—and such pride in the area. Poplars would have been his home, and his sense of possessiveness was tangible. And his family would have been looked after all that time by *her* mother! With a rush of emotion Melody realised that he would have known Frances, even though he'd apparently not lived at Poplars much since childhood.

The information that she'd just been given had left Melody feeling dry-mouthed and slightly taken aback. Yet why? she asked herself. Wasn't she here to find out things—about herself, about her mother's past? Perhaps these were two little pieces of the jigsaw of her life which had to be fitted in first. And maybe that would be it. Maybe there was nothing more of significance to learn.

She shivered slightly, and Fee looked at her sharply. 'You're not *cold*, are you, Mel?' she said. 'In this heat?'

'No—no, of course not.'

'Um, well…I hope you aren't sickening for something—there's a summer flu going around at the moment.'

Mel smiled quickly. 'I'm fine, Fee, honestly,' she said.

But somehow she wasn't really fine. She felt disturbed—and she knew the reason. Adam Carlisle had emerged from out of nowhere, and his family had had a direct influence on her mother's life. Despite all her best intentions, his presence was affecting her feelings in the sort of way she'd thought she was immune from for ever.

# CHAPTER FOUR

DECIDING that there was no time like the present, Melody wanted to make an immediate start. So presently, having gone back to Poplars to change into her jeans, she allowed Adam to drive her into the village to make some purchases. He had already established that the electrics were all in working order, and that the cottage's hot water system—after a few false starts—was functioning perfectly well. So now all they needed were some basic cleaning materials.

Adam pulled up outside the post office, which seemed to double up as a general store, and together they went inside, selecting a long-handled broom, dustpan and brush, two buckets, scrubbing brushes and floor cloths, and various cleaning fluids. Fee had tried to insist that they borrow everything from Poplars, but Melody had been adamant that she was going to need it all for the long term, so there was no point.

As they piled their purchases into the car Melody felt an almost childish thrill at the thought of the mundane task ahead. Cleaning might not be everyone's idea of fun, she thought, but when it was your very own place—empty, to do with what you liked—it became a more attractive prospect. And she was honest enough to admit that sitting there beside Adam as he drove them back was adding its own very particular dimension!

Although his unexpected interest in her and her acquisition of the cottage might have struck her as rather annoying at first, Melody now found herself grateful that she wasn't entirely alone. And he did seem genuinely anxious to help her. She shrugged inwardly—maybe he *was* getting bored with his long holiday, and with pleasing himself with nothing much to do. It was true, she reflected, that a prolonged period of inactivity with no particular focus could pall after a while.

She glanced across at him covertly. He had the most amazingly masculine profile she'd ever seen on a man... It had an almost carved look about it, perfect and symmetrical, with a very firm chin which might indicate a ruthless streak, perhaps? And every time she'd had the full benefit of his glittering eyes looking down at her she had been conscious of being almost wrapped up in his gaze—enfolded, momentarily held prisoner. She turned to look out of the window, thinking that the last few days seemed to be part of an unimaginable dream—a dream from which she didn't want to wake up!

Back at the cottage, they took everything inside and began taking stock.

'Of course I shall have the whole place redecorated,' Melody announced. 'I know a very good team in London—they did our flat—and they won't object to spending a week or two down here on this.' She glanced up at Adam, who she knew had been watching her. 'Unless Callum knows of local workmen who'd appreciate the opportunity?' she added, bending to pick up the packet which held the rubber gloves they'd bought.

'Well, we could ask him,' Adam said. He paused. 'If that is your intention why are we bothering to clean up here now? Can't we leave it all to the decorators?'

'Of course not,' Melody said at once. 'If we get the place reasonably clean and fresh it'll give them a start, and more incentive to make a really good job of it. I don't intend to pay the sort of rates these people charge for the simple task of cleaning up—something I can do quite well myself.' She looked away for a second. 'But you don't have to be involved, Adam. Honestly…I can cope by myself.'

'Don't be silly,' he replied shortly. 'I told you—I want to help.' He picked up the broom which had been leaning against the wall. 'Now, I propose we start upstairs and work our way down—or would you like it the other way around?'

Melody smiled up at him, relieved that he was going to stay. Although the cottage was not large, it was going to take some time to clean it thoroughly—and two pairs of hands were better than one. 'No—I agree,' she said lightly. 'Let's begin upstairs.'

As the back bedroom was the largest, it was decided that they should begin on that. Adam went into the bathroom to fill one of the buckets with hot water, adding some frothy detergent, while Melody began sweeping, dragging the broom from ceiling to floor, getting into the cornices and corners, painfully aware of the countless cobwebs she was disturbing. The dust was already beginning to make her nose tingle, and as Adam returned with the heavy bucket she sneezed violently, three or four times in quick succession. He grinned across at her.

'Bless you and bless you,' he said. He paused. 'I don't hold out much hope for your white T-shirt,' he added.

'Doesn't matter. I've packed plenty of spares,' Melody said nonchalantly, continuing with her brushing.

They'd thrown the window wide open, and the blessed summer air, filtering into the room, went some way towards giving it a more wholesome feel. When Adam, on his hands and knees, began scrubbing the floor furiously, Melody began to feel that truly this was her home. Home! What a wonderful thought! Because this place, even in its present state, felt more like home than the flat in London ever had, she realised. And she was aware that in wanting to clean it, to literally touch and handle every part of it, she was linking herself with her own life-blood, her own destiny. And her hard-working mother's spirit seemed to inhabit the place, fill it with her presence, which made Melody's heart glow.

She pulled herself away from this rather intense train of thought and watched Adam for a moment or two, noted his strong muscles tensing and flexing beneath the tanned skin on his arms as he squeezed water from the cloth he was using. As he continued with what he was doing his casual top pulled away from the waist of his jeans, exposing a band of lean, supple body which hardened and rippled with the effort, and beads of perspiration glistened on the back of his neck...

Impulsively, Melody crouched down beside him for a second, a surge of gratefulness overcoming any shyness she might have felt. 'Adam—it's—I mean—it's so good of you to be doing this,' she said earnestly. 'Why should you be spending time on my behalf? I mean—we hardly know each other, and scrubbing out a grubby property is hardly the stuff of a dream holiday, is it?'

He stopped for a moment and leaned back on his heels, looking at her squarely. 'In some people's view it might be the stuff of nightmares,' he agreed amiably. 'But don't worry about it, Mel.' He paused. 'I never do anything I don't want to do— and, as I told you, I like a challenge. And anyway...' he hesitated briefly '...if this was now Callum and Fee's place I'd probably be doing it for them.'

Melody shrank back. It was easy to forget that her successful bid for the cottage had spoiled his friends' plans. His *best* friends' plans. She couldn't rid herself of the feeling that she'd committed an act of felony.

She stood up quickly. 'There isn't any more I can do here,' she said. 'So I'll go and suss out the bathroom.'

He didn't look up, or make any comment, and Melody went

across the narrow landing. Staring around her, she noted that all the porcelain must have been replaced in the not-too-distant past—although an ugly brown stain in the bath, running from the taps to the plug, would need some serious attention. She put her head on one side pensively. She'd probably have this—her very favourite room in any house—refitted at some point. But it certainly wasn't bad enough to consider that now. Rome wasn't built in a day, she reminded herself.

Going over to the handbasin, she opened the window wide and leaned out, resting her arms on the sill, glorying in the vision of her somewhat overgrown garden. Those gooseberry bushes, with the fruit luscious and turning pink with ripeness, were begging to be stripped, she thought.

Suddenly something large and black fell directly down past her line of vision, brushing her nose and chin as it went straight down the front of her T-shirt, which had gaped open at the neck. Melody's heart jumped right into her mouth and she let out a scream of pure terror as she pulled at her top in anguish. 'Aaaaargh!' she yelled. 'Oh, no—no—*help*!'

There was an almighty crash from the bedroom as Adam's feet obviously made contact with the side of his bucket, and almost at once he was beside her, grabbing her by the arm. 'What the hell's wrong?' he demanded savagely.

By this time Melody had ripped off her top, flinging it on the floor, and just stood there, literally shaking from head to foot. 'Something…something *horrible*…has just fallen down my neck!' she cried, desperately trying to control herself, and failing miserably. 'Oh God, Adam… It was *disgusting*!'

He stared at her for a minute, trying to suppress a grin. 'Well…I thought you were being murdered,' he said, trying to unlock his gaze from Melody's low-cut lacy bra, which enhanced the perfect shape and roundness of her dainty figure and delectable cleavage. He turned away decisively and picked up her shirt, shaking it out vigorously. At once a massive spider ran across the room in a frenzied effort to escape. When she saw it, Melody fought to control another shudder of horror.

'Ugh…that's…horrible—*horrible*! I cannot stand spiders!' she cried. 'Or anything with more than two legs! Oh, Adam… that was *awful*!'

She was still trembling, and for a moment he thought she was going to burst into tears. Part of him wanted to take her by the shoulders and shake her, tell her not to be so ridiculous, but he was aware that for some people the fear of insects—especially spiders—was not something minor which could easily be controlled. Like any phobia, it must be treated with consideration. He knew that.

He put his arm around her waist and gently drew her towards him. The feel of her scantily clad body next to his sent his male instincts soaring wildly. He swallowed, wishing that his hands didn't smell of disinfectant—though that did have the effect of helping him to calm his momentary lust. 'It's okay, Mel…don't worry. The thing's gone now—disappeared,' he said reasonably. 'You know they're much more frightened of you than you can ever be of them,' he murmured into her ear.

'I don't care!' she repeated. 'They move so fast…and they *bite*!'

'Oh, not all of them bite—' Adam began, but she interrupted.

'I know someone who was bitten—or stung—I don't care which. Her arm became infected and she was on antibiotics for *weeks*!' Melody leaned right into him now, as he held her, but soon she began to calm down, her breathing becoming steadier. She turned and looked up into his face. 'Oh, dear…I'm sorry— really,' she said at last. 'I'm not proud of my behaviour… You must think I'm a fool, Adam…'

'Of course I don't,' he said coolly. 'Fear of spiders is a well-known phenomenon.' He paused. 'There are groups that can help, you know,' he went on. 'Help with any hang-up.' He didn't let her go, only too aware of the thudding of his heart against her breasts.

After a few seconds she pulled away. 'I'm sorry,' she repeated, 'I think I overreacted…but I really couldn't help it…'

'Don't apologise,' he said. 'You're not the only person in the world who's afraid of creepy crawlies.'

He knew that the spider was not the thing uppermost in his mind at that moment! How had he stopped himself from kissing her? he wondered. Because he *almost* had done. He had wanted to, in a moment of madness—and she'd not yanked herself away either, as she might easily have done.

Adam still had her T-shirt tucked under his arm, and he held it out to her. 'Are you going to put this back on?' he enquired, and she shuddered.

'Certainly not,' she said. 'But I'd like to go back to Poplars and put on something fresh.'

He looked down at her quizzically. Perhaps this was the moment to point out that if she did intend to be a country-dweller—even if it was on a part-time basis—she'd better get used to unwelcome company now and then

'There are no guarantees regarding spiders, woodlice *et al*,' he said, as they went down the stairs. 'Not in any cottage. Certainly not in one of this age. They come with the territory, I'm afraid, Mel.'

'Oh, you can buy stuff to deter them,' Melody replied quickly, having by now reasserted her self-control. 'Perhaps they'll all eventually get the message,' she added hopefully.

'Don't count on it,' Adam said enigmatically. 'It would be wiser to try and develop a more rational frame of mind, so that when you do come across anything you can handle it. You can get used to anything—if you persist,' he added.

Melody wasn't convinced by this argument, and she bit her

lip, angry with herself, and a bit piqued at the advice he was dishing out—especially as she knew that he was right. That spider would not be the only thing she'd come across in the future…in fact there was probably much worse to come—rats, even! she thought. But sitting beside Adam now, as he drove slowly back up the drive of Poplars, she felt her optimism begin bubbling back to the surface of her thoughts. She loved it— *loved* it—that the cottage was hers!

She didn't look across at Adam as he drew into the car park. She didn't need to look at him, because the drift of his maleness touched her nostrils, made her realise with a jolt what had been wrenched from her life when Crispin had been killed. Her husband had been the last man to touch her, to hold her in that certain way that needed no explanation, and when she'd felt Adam's arms around her just now it had evoked a physical need in her that she'd thought she'd filed away for ever. Hadn't she vowed that her one serious relationship was to be her last? That she would never expose herself to the trauma of loss ever again? Yet a man whom she barely knew had just driven a horse and cart through that determination!

She chided herself angrily at her weakness. It must be this unusually warm summer weather, plus the heady experience of spending all that money on her idyllic home in the country which was ruffling her normally level-headed and practical thinking. Well, that was her story, and she'd stick to it!

She got out of the car, and ran quickly up the stairs to her room. Fortunately there was no one about, and she shut the door behind her gratefully.

For a few moments she sat on the edge of the bed, where she had a good view of herself in the wall mirror. The face that stared back at her didn't seem like hers—more like that of someone she'd once known.

Snap out of this daydreaming, she told herself sharply, going over to the chest of drawers for a fresh T-shirt. Keep your eye on the ball! Just because she'd been held closely by a man— for the first time in more than a year—it hadn't changed a thing. That incident in the life of someone like Adam would have been a well-practised passing fancy. What he'd said on that first evening, about not being married, nor apparently wishing to be, left her in no doubt that his interest in the opposite sex was purely physical—and transitory. Holding her like that hadn't been anything more than a consoling gesture to a stupid female who was scared of spiders. He would have forgotten about it already.

She shrugged on the clean top, releasing her long hair from the back in a faintly irritable gesture…well, then, *she'd* better forget all about it, too!

Waiting for her outside, Adam couldn't believe that, yet again, he was allowing himself to be beguiled by a beautiful woman. Hadn't the lesson he'd thought he'd learned been harsh enough? It was true that he'd found her attractive from the moment he'd set eyes on her, but it had never been his intention to let his feelings be stirred in any way at all. Yet this morning had shattered his confidence in that determination, because for those few seconds he'd not only wanted her, he'd recognised that deeper, familiar longing, which spelt danger. Of course he'd dated many women since the break-up with Lucy, but they'd meant nothing—nothing at all. And that was the way he wanted it.

His lip curled slightly as he recalled Melody's horror at that creature running down her cleavage. Well, as he'd told her, she'd better get used to such things. Together with everything else that went with living in a place like this—however infrequent her visits were to be. No smart shops, no theatres or museums to alleviate boredom on wet weekends, to keep a city girl amused.

He leaned forward on the steering wheel, resting his chin on his hands for a moment. Why was the woman getting to him anyway? Why was he bothering to think about her like this? Something about her told him that as soon as she returned to London, Gatehouse Cottage would take a very back seat in her mind. He felt, overwhelmingly, that her purchase had been a rush of blood to the head of someone who had far too much money at her disposal. After all, why would anyone—any normal person—buy a property in the country without a second thought? Without apparently having had any idea that such a thing might occur in the first place? It didn't make any sense.

He glanced out of the window to see her coming towards him. She smiled at him as their eyes met, and he leaned across to open the passenger door for her. Why did this woman look so delectable? he asked himself. And why had their paths had to cross?

# CHAPTER FIVE

THE following morning Melody woke early, conscious of the sun filtering through the slightly parted curtains at her window. She smiled to herself. It was going to be yet another fine, warm day.

She lay on her back for a moment, staring up at the ceiling. She and Adam had spent almost all of yesterday spring-cleaning the cottage, and when they'd packed up finally she had felt as if an almost spiritual event had occurred. It was hard for her to explain it, even to herself, but by cleaning away the dust and grime of the lives of other occupants she felt that she was now ready for new beginnings.

She'd been dog-tired by the time they'd called it a day, and although Adam had suggested that they go somewhere for supper Melody had declined the offer. 'All I need now is a long, warm bath and an early night,' she'd said.

Anyway, the picnic lunch Fee had brought down for them—soft rolls with ham and cheese, fruit and coffee, plus a cool bag containing ice-cold drinks—had kept them going all day. Melody had certainly not had sufficient appetite to bother dressing up and going out somewhere to eat. As they'd put all the cleaning things neatly in the kitchen cupboard, Adam's response to her refusal had been non-committal.

'Okay. Fine by me,' was all he'd said.

Now, Melody jumped out of bed decisively. It was not even seven a.m. yet. There was plenty of time to go for a walk across the fields before breakfast—which she was in the habit of having at about eight or nine o'clock.

Washing quickly, she selected cream trousers and a turquoise cotton top, then stooped down for her running shoes, fixing the straps firmly. She and Adam had parted company yesterday without any reference to today, and Melody hoped that he wouldn't feel under any obligation to go on taking her under his wing. She'd been more than grateful for all his efforts yesterday—and had told him so, over and over again—but for the time being there was little more to be done at the cottage, so he had no need to interrupt his holiday further on her behalf.

She bit her lip. This could be awkward for both of them, she thought. She did not want to feel obligated to him, but neither did she want to give him the brush-off—not after all he'd done yesterday. And equally, she thought, he might feel that he couldn't very well stop what he'd started and abandon her to her own devices. Melody brushed out her hair vigorously and pulled it back in a ponytail. Stop worrying, she told herself. Things will pan out. Anyway, first things first. This early walk was the next important thing on her agenda.

The front door was already wide open—Callum and Fee's day had obviously begun—and she could hear muffled voices from the kitchen as she went outside. She stood quite still for a moment, taking in lungfuls of fresh air. She could already feel the life-enhancing effect of not inhaling toxic fumes from countless streams of traffic. Lap it up while you can, she told herself. All too soon she'd be back in the smoke.

Thinking along these lines made her realise that she probably ought to ring the office at some point—she'd neither made nor received any calls on her holiday from her colleagues, and the thought of her long break coming to an end, of having to leave her cottage, filled her with a silly sense of homesickness. How daft could you be? she asked herself. The next time she returned here the place would still be standing. Nothing was going to happen to it. And anyway, before that she had some fruit-picking to do. She'd take as much of the stuff back with her as she could manage, to distribute among her workmates...

She wondered what their reaction would be to her news. She imagined that they'd all be mildly surprised—her purchase was hardly the equivalent of a few sticks of rock, or a locally crafted souvenir, she thought, smiling briefly. But her closest colleagues—Eve and Jon, who'd lived together for ages—*they'd* be more than interested! Their main preoccupation outside work seemed to be looking at properties. She'd ring them tomorrow and tell them, Melody thought. Keeping her news to herself seemed unnecessarily secretive.

She set off rapidly, taking the long track behind Poplars towards a bank of trees she could see in the near distance. The turf was soft and mossy beneath her feet, and Melody felt that she could walk for miles with no trouble at all. Presently she came to a stile at the foot of a hilly area, and, climbing over it easily, she began making her way upwards, wondering what she'd see when she reached the top. When she did, she wasn't disappointed. Below her the overgrown fields fell away on either side, and the whole undulating scene represented a picture-book vision of flowering bushes and wild plants. She could see scores of poppies, cow-parsley everywhere, and beneath her feet bright buttercups and dandelions, adding their own vivid glory as they vied for attention. The air—like champagne—was filled with the hum of bees, already on their hunt for nectar.

Melody's heart missed a beat. How many times had Frances told her about her countless expeditions to collect blossom and foliage to decorate Poplars—and her own, humbler dwelling?

And, as if to complete this idyllic picture, Melody espied a small stream, meandering along the bottom of the field. Starting to make her way down, she was forced to run as her feet gathered pace, her cheeks beginning to redden with the effort. When she reached the stream, she saw that thanks to the long spell of hot weather the water was no more than a trickle, but the effect of sunlight on moving water was pure magic. Melody breathed in deeply, feeling at that moment that she must be the luckiest person in the world.

Nimbly, she stepped over the stream and went towards the bushes in front of her. She could see at a glance that there were suitable things to pick—even though she'd probably have to endure pinched fingers in the process!

She'd barely begun to make her selection when Adam's voice, almost immediately behind her, made her jump. Turning quickly, she saw him standing a few feet away, his hands in his pockets, a faint smile on his lips.

'So…you're a countryside pilferer, are you?' he said, and without waiting for a reply added, 'Why are you up so early? After all you did yesterday I thought you'd be asleep until lunchtime.'

She stood back. 'Oh—well, I had a very early night,' she said. 'And I certainly wasn't going to waste this lovely morning.' She stared up at him. He was wearing chinos, and a light open-neck shirt, and his black hair shone like polished coal in the sunlight. She turned away. 'Anyway—what are *you* doing up and about?' she asked.

'Oh, I take the dogs out first thing,' he said, not taking his eyes from her, and thinking how sweet and natural she looked. So different from his first impression at the auction. And she'd surprised him yesterday, with how she'd worked at the cottage.

She'd insisted on scrubbing every inch of the bathroom by herself—which had been no mean feat, because it had been the grimiest room in the place. And there'd been no complaints, no expecting to go back to Poplars for a rest, and she hadn't checked her appearance in the mirror either—rather unusual in a woman, he thought, or at any rate in the women he'd known all his life.

'What have you done with Tam and Millie, then?' she asked, glancing around her.

'Oh, they're enjoying themselves sniffing about in that copse over there,' he replied. He gave one short, sharp whistle through his teeth, and at once both animals emerged and ambled up towards them, going over to Melody to be made a fuss of.

She glanced up at Adam. 'Is it…will it be okay for me to pick a few bits and pieces from these bushes?' she asked. 'They're not all protected species, are they?'

'Shouldn't think so,' he said casually. 'Help yourself. The owners are very gracious people. They like the locals to enjoy their property, as long as it's respected.'

'Who *does* own all this, then?' Melody asked curiously.

'It belongs to the big house about a mile thataway,' Adam said, indicating behind him. 'The de Wintons own it now. The family is filthy rich, but lovely with it, and since this area is not suitable for farming it's mostly a local amenity.'

Melody turned back to the bushes. There'd be no point in picking too much, but a modest arrangement in a tumbler on her bedroom cabinet would satisfy a particular need—though they wouldn't last long. She knew that. Not like the exotic blooms Adam had given her.

He threw himself down on the grass and leaned back on one elbow, gazing up at her as she foraged around, her smooth brown arms raised, her head held high, the ponytail trailing luxuriously down her back.

'Finding anything spectacular?' he enquired, wishing again that this woman wasn't quite so attractive to look at. He kept remembering the feel of her feminine curves pressed into his chest. He shook himself briefly. This long sunny spell had gone right to his head!

'Everything's spectacular,' she replied without looking around. 'I mean, just *look* at this dog-rose…such a dainty pink. I must have just a small sprig—if I can manage to snap a bit off. Ow!' she said, sucking a finger noisily.

Adam immediately got up. 'Here—let me,' he said, coming over to stand next to her.

Melody stood back as he leaned upwards and snapped off a stem. He turned to look down at her and, swallowing, she moved away from him quickly. There was no need for them to be *that* close! 'That's fine, Adam…thanks,' she said, taking the cluster of roses from him. She shaded her eyes from the sun for a moment. 'There are lots of other things over there,' she said. 'And those daisies are so long-stemmed—I must have some of those!' She scrambled past him for a moment. 'But I must not allow myself to get carried away!' she added.

With both dogs flopping down beside him, Adam resumed his prone position on the grass and watched her idly. Presently she stood back and examined the quite considerable amount of foliage she was holding in her arms.

'There—that will do,' she said, glancing down at him.

He waited for a second before speaking, then, 'Come and sit down,' he said, patting the ground beside him.

Melody did as she was told, feeling light-hearted—and light-headed!

He leaned towards her so that they were almost touching, and, looking down briefly at the flowers, said, 'Well, what have you got there, Mel? Have you any idea what you've been picking?' he asked.

She returned his glance, interpreting what he'd just said as criticism of a townie who was more used to expensive florists' shops than dusty hedgerows! She held the bunch away from her and pointed with her forefinger. 'Let me enlighten you,' she said coolly. 'Here we have foxgloves—which will look well with the meadowsweet and the daisies—together with gorgeous stems of honeysuckle. Just smell those—don't they make your mouth water? This dainty blue flower I'm pretty sure is meadow cranesbill, and here we have ladies' smock—a bit gangly, but still charming—and of course the ubiquitous Queen Charlotte's lace—known to you, no doubt, as cow parsley. And—'

'Stop, stop!' Adam said. 'I'm impressed! Where did all that knowledge come from? You've obviously studied the subject…'

She shot him a quick glance. 'Not exactly,' she said. 'But my mother used to talk to me about flowers a lot, show me pictures. And her favourite pastime was to paint—she did beautiful still-life watercolours, which will be hung on my cottage walls eventually.' She paused. 'She even gave me a jigsaw puzzle once, with all the names of flowers, wild and cultivated. We did that together for hours. So it was just something I learned at my mother's knee, you might say.' She looked away for a second. Should she tell Adam how closely she was connected to the place—how, in a way, she was so closely connected to *him*, or at any rate to Poplars and Gatehouse Cottage?

The moment passed and she said nothing, for she still felt this need to guard Frances's secret. But the longer it went on, the more difficult it would become. She knew that. She shrugged inwardly. Maybe there would be no need to tell him, or anyone, why she had felt a pressing need to own the cottage, or why she already felt an integral part of the village. So much time had gone by, she thought wistfully. Her mother's world was a different one from the one in which *she* was now living.

Adam leaned forward, hugging his knees and staring ahead of him at the barely moving water of the stream a foot or two away from them. This woman was beginning to confuse him.

He'd always prided himself that he was good at first impressions, that he could sum someone up straight away. But there was a lot about Mel that defied his former assessment. She didn't seem quite the indulged rich-kid who'd plucked Gatehouse Cottage from under their noses—more that she genuinely wanted to be part of the place. To live it.

'You've put me to shame,' he said, not looking at her. 'I was born here—my parents once owned Poplars, as a matter of fact—and as a young child I used to tramp these fields, but I was never particularly interested in flora and fauna. Certainly not enough to learn about them. Then I was packed off to boarding school at nine, after which university…so my childhood memories are slight.' He paused. 'But there must be something about one's early childhood, because I feel a need—a compulsion—to keep returning each year. And of course the biggest excuse is to spend time with Callum and Fee, who've always remained my best friends.'

There was a silence before Melody said lightly, 'Well, then, it must be like coming home each time.'

She didn't say that Fee had already told her some of this, because that would have looked as if they'd been gossiping about him. So it was just another secret! She was good at secrets, she thought.

Neither of them said anything then, and after a few moments Melody, feeling her feet throbbing, slipped her shoes off and inched herself forward, dipping her toes into the stream. 'Oh…that's *so* good,' she breathed, glancing back over her shoulder at Adam.

He grinned back at her. 'I've never seen the water this low,' he said. 'It's barely covering your feet.'

'No, I know—but it's doing the job,' Melody replied. She wiggled her toes for a few moments, then sat back for the sun to dry her off. 'I shall relive all this when I get back to London,' she said. 'It'll be a whole world away.'

Adam looked at her thoughtfully. 'So—when d'you expect to be returning?' he asked, in a casual tone which he might have used to anyone as a polite enquiry.

'Can't be sure just yet,' Melody replied, leaning back on her elbows to bring her down to lounge alongside him. 'It'll all depend on work, of course. But I shall make immediate plans to engage the decorators.' Her eyes shone as she anticipated the time ahead, and she turned to see him gazing at her. 'I must take lots of photographs of the cottage later, of every room, so that I'll have something to show them. It'll give them an idea.' She paused. 'And then it'll be measuring up for carpets and curtains.' She closed her eyes briefly. 'D'you know, I feel exactly as I did when I was given my first dolls' house! Arranging everything to suit just *me*!'

A pulse twitched and hardened in Adam's neck as he continued looking at her. He knew that if he didn't break the spell this woman was weaving around him he wouldn't be able to stop himself from gathering her up in his arms and claiming her mouth. At that moment, sitting here with birdsong all around them, he knew that he wanted to possess her—really possess her—and he only just managed to restrain himself. He recalled the feel of her as she'd clutched him in that grimy bathroom yesterday, as she'd rested her head against his shoulder for that brief second—though you could hardly call that a come-on, he thought. He was used to the women he knew seizing an opportunity like that with both hands! But he'd been surprised, and cross with himself, at how she'd stirred him… Women were not to be trusted—he knew that better than anyone. Yet here he was, at it again! Allowing himself to be aroused by a beautiful, intelligent female—and, worst of all, by a woman whose arrival in the village had upset his plans!

All at once Melody seemed to sense the sudden emotional tenseness between them, and she stood up quickly, her heart-beat beginning to notch up noticeably. Spending time with the devilishly handsome Adam Carlisle had not been part of her holiday plan! If she couldn't shake him off soon it was going to confuse everything. Buying a property in the country was enough of an event on its own. Don't let things get complicated, she warned herself. Yet every time his dark eyes looked into hers in that very special way they seemed to penetrate her soul, holding her captive. But she knew that she'd always felt things deeply—too deeply—and she did not want to risk being hurt again. To risk losing again.

When her mother had died it had seemed the end of her world for a while. Then fate had dealt her another blow, when Crispin had been killed, and she'd shed enough tears to float a boat. Well, she'd made up her mind never to be asked to pay such a price for happiness again.

Quickly she thrust on her trainers and got to her feet, glancing down at Adam briefly, knowing that he'd wanted to kiss her, and knowing that she'd got *that* close to letting him do it. 'I think I must go back for some breakfast,' she said, matter-of-factly. 'The time has just flown by…'

He got up, too, then, and without another word fell into step beside her as she walked on rapidly, the dogs trotting happily in front of them. Once or twice she stumbled over the rough ground, and Adam automatically put a hand under her elbow to steady her. But, not wanting to feel the touch of his hand, not wanting to feel any part of him close to her, she deliberately moved away quickly, almost shrugging him off.

He knew her motive, and shook his head briefly as he looked down at her. 'I just don't want you to sprain an ankle,' he said shortly. 'We've some way to go yet, and even your weight might be too much.'

'Oh, don't worry,' Melody replied. 'I shan't expect any special favours. I'll get back under my own steam whatever happens. I promise you that.'

'Oh, I don't doubt that you're fully self-contained, Mel,' he said. 'But if you've ever tried walking with a sprained ankle you'll know what I'm talking about. You'd be lucky to get back to Poplars by bedtime, never mind breakfast.'

'Has it ever happened to you, then?' Melody asked.

'Yes. Playing rugby,' he replied. 'I thought I could get off the pitch unaided, but I was wrong. And I've never forgotten the pain.'

'D'you play a lot?' Melody asked, glad of the neutral conversation.

'Not now,' he said shortly. 'It's a young man's game.'

She looked up at him, thinking that his face bore no testimonies to the game—no misshapen nose or lumpy ears to spoil his model features.

They made good time getting back to Poplars—Melody still clutching her precious blooms, which even now were beginning to wilt slightly.

'I must put these in water and have a wash,' she said lightly, before running quickly up the stairs to her room. Adam merely nodded as they parted company.

Looking around her, Melody could see that there was nothing remotely suitable to arrange her flowers in, so presently she filled the washbasin with cold water and laid all the foliage in it up to the neck, realising that she'd need to ask Fee for a vase or jar.

She paused for a moment in front of the mirror, idly ruffling her fingers through her fringe. She was starving by now, but wanted to give Adam time to have his own breakfast before going down. She didn't want it to become the norm for them to spend all their time together, but that was how it seemed to be turning out. It was still not much after nine, but she didn't want to hold Fee up any longer. She'd noticed before that the other guests all tended to eat early, so she'd probably be the last one in the dining room again, she thought.

At about a quarter past nine she ventured downstairs. The large, inviting room was empty, with only one table—hers, obviously—still laid up for breakfast. Adam must have swallowed his pretty quickly, she thought, going over to the large side table which still had all the cereals and fruit displayed.

She poured herself a glass of orange juice, and put a small helping of muesli into a bowl, then filled a generous cup with coffee from the percolator which was bubbling alongside.

As she went to sit down Callum emerged, a sunny smile on his broad features. 'Morning, Mel,' he said. 'Enjoyed your early walk? Adam told me he'd bumped into you. Perfect morning again, isn't it?'

Melody returned his smile. 'It is,' she agreed. 'I can't believe my luck!'

'Yes, we've got very satisfied guests at the moment. But it does rain here—I can promise you that—and it often goes on for days!'

'Well, so long as it behaves itself for a little while longer,' Melody said, sitting down and unfolding her napkin.

'Now—full English, Mel?' Callum asked.

Melody smiled. 'I don't think so, thanks. But a soft-boiled egg and some toast would be great, Callum.' She paused. 'No Fee today?' she asked lightly.

A brief frown crossed the man's face for a second. 'She's…she's having a bit of a lie-down for an hour,' he said. 'Not feeling too good… It's this heat, I think.' He turned abruptly. 'One soft-boiled egg, coming up.'

He left the room and Melody stared after him, remembering her conversation with Fee yesterday and hoping that it *was* only the heat affecting the girl, and not anything more sinister. She'd known the couple for such a short time, yet it was impossible not to warm to them…they were so kind and generous. Adam certainly thought so, and clearly valued their friendship.

Just thinking of the man seemed to conjure him up.

Suddenly he appeared at the door, going over to fill a large mug with coffee before coming across to sit down opposite her.

'Mind if I join you?' he said—though it wasn't a question, more a declaration of intent! 'Have you found anything suitable to put your morning's harvest in?' he asked.

'No,' Melody replied. 'But that jug in the window over there would be perfect. D'you think they'd mind if I borrowed it?'

'Oh, we'll take it and ask later,' Adam said cheerfully, knowing full well that Fee never objected to anything.

Melody tried not to mind that he'd turned up. Even though she'd decided that for the rest of the day she was going to give him a wide berth. 'Have you had breakfast?' she asked, looking up at him over the rim of her glass of juice.

'I grabbed a slice of toast a few minutes ago,' he replied easily. 'As a matter of fact the three of us went over to the Rose & Crown for supper last night, and ate rather well. So it's no hardship to go without this morning.' He paused. 'You should have come with us.'

He studied her closely as she dipped her spoon into the muesli and began to eat, thinking what a graceful woman she was. Everything she did—eating, or gathering flowers from the hedges, or scrubbing discoloured pipes in the cottage—she seemed to do with a kind of unassuming elegance. He pursed his lips and stared out of the window. In a couple of weeks she'd have gone home to London and he'd be on his way back to the Far East. He grimaced inwardly at the thought. He didn't want to go back—well, he *never* wanted to go back. He wanted to stay here!

'I was much too tired to eat,' Melody said. 'I get to a certain point when sleep is the only answer for me.'

She finished the muesli just as Callum came back with her boiled egg, and Adam leaned back in his chair nonchalantly, looking up.

'Can we use your computer later, Callum?' he asked. 'Mel wants some pictures of the cottage. I've got my digital camera, and I thought we'd go down there later and take some. Then we could print off some copies for her to take back with her.'

'Course you can,' Callum said at once. 'Be my guest!'

Melody looked across at Adam. It was no good. The man was making himself useful again—*too* useful—and it was becoming impossible for her to refuse him! But she had to admit that the arrangement he was suggesting would be very convenient—and her own camera was not digital.

Presently, back in her room, she arranged her bouquet of wild flowers in the wide-necked jug she'd borrowed, and placed them on the windowsill. To her, they were as perfect as the bouquet which Adam had presented her with. She paused for a moment or two, her thoughts—as usual—on their normal helter-skelter of emotion. When she'd booked this holiday she could never have guessed what lay ahead—that she would buy the very home in which her beloved mother had lived, and in which she'd given birth to her only child. Nor that she would tread probably the very path that her mother had wandered along and pluck the same sort of flowers… Melody had the feeling that her existence was taking on a life of its own, and the most dramatic part of it was that in the midst of it all she knew she'd met the most breathtakingly gorgeous man she was ever likely to set eyes on! And his apparent determination to be constantly by her side was upsetting her equilibrium!

She sat for a moment on the edge of her bed, her hands clasped in her lap. Warning bells were beginning to ring. Don't get involved any further with him, she instructed herself anxiously. Think of something—anything—some excuse—to put distance between you. If you don't, it will all end in tears—and they'll be *your* tears!

That thought brought Melody to a sudden decision, and,

leaning across to her bedside table, she picked up her mobile and made a phone call. After a few minutes' conversation with the person on the other end she snapped it shut, a small glint of satisfaction in her eyes. Well, that might go some way to cooling things down a bit, she thought. If Adam Carlisle thought that he was going to be unelected Master of Ceremonies in her life he was going to be disappointed!

## CHAPTER SIX

'I THINK those shots of the cottage that we took this morning will come out well,' Adam said lazily. 'I'll print them off later, and we can chuck any you don't think you'll need.'

He'd discarded his shirt and was lying full-stretch on the warm sand, his hands clasped behind his head. He turned to look at Melody as he spoke.

Half-sitting next to him, she tried not to be too aware of his brown muscular chest, with the dark line of strong body hair reaching down to the waist of his jeans, and she looked away, concentrating on the line of the horizon instead. The sheer expanse of blue water beyond them was dotted with what looked like millions of tiny diamonds, shifting and dazzling as the sunlight danced on the waves.

In spite of all her good intentions, his suggested visit to this secluded cove was, she had to admit, an unexpected treat. She'd only been to the seaside once or twice so far on her holiday, and she hadn't known that this place existed. Although they were certainly not the only ones there, it was blissfully unpopulated. Their nearest neighbours were an elderly man and his dog, and, a bit further away, a young couple with a baby.

'D'you think that not many people know about this beach?' Melody asked curiously.

'Oh, I'm sure it's known,' Adam replied casually. 'But of course there's absolutely nothing here but sea and sand... No ice-cream vans, or shops selling the gaudy stuff that most people seem to need. Actually,' he added, 'it used to be a private beach, owned by a titled family who lived in a big house nearby which no longer exists.'

He turned to look at her as he spoke. She had changed earlier, into a honey-coloured sundress, with fine spaghetti straps that exposed the perfect contours of her neck and shoulders and was cut just low enough to reveal a glimpse of her curvaceous figure. It could hardly be described as a provocative number, he thought briefly, but it did plenty to excite *his* interest. Especially as she seemed unusually uninhibited about letting the sun reach her thighs, and had drawn her skirt up so that the sun could reach the length of her slender, fine-skinned legs.

'Well, it's just another little piece of paradise, as far as I'm concerned,' Melody said, deciding that she wasn't going to waste a single moment of the afternoon feeling that yet again she'd been manipulated. She and Adam had spent most of the morning taking dozens of shots of the cottage and garden—and he'd also recommended that they should start picking some of the fruit.

'It'll take us some time to do it,' he'd said, and Melody had sighed inwardly at the 'us'. She'd have been more than content to go it alone. Anyway, she'd thought, wasn't it high time for him to be returning to the Far East? Surely they must be missing his fantastic organisation skills by now? Although she couldn't deny that she was starting to enjoy the time they spent together immensely.

'It was a shame that Fee couldn't come with us after all,' she said now, for his suggestion that they should go to the coast had included the other woman as well. That had been the main— the *only*—reason Melody had accepted the invitation. There was safety in numbers, and she'd have loved to have Fee's cheerful company. Yet once again she and Adam were to be a cosy couple.

'Yes, I'm really sorry about that,' he replied—without much conviction. 'She would have enjoyed a couple of hours away from the unremitting toil, and the sea air would have done her good. But there you go. At the last minute she didn't feel up to it, so Callum said.' There was silence for a few moments, then, 'Are you going to join me for a swim?' he asked. 'The tide's just right now, and the water is calm… There's never much opportunity for surfing, if that's your preference,' he added.

In answer, Melody turned to rummage in her brightly coloured holdall. 'Calm water will be perfect for me,' she said. 'I've only tried surfing once, and I wasn't all that good at it to tell you the truth.' She pulled out her swimming things and stood up. Adam grinned up at her.

'Feel free,' he murmured smoothly. 'I'll be gallant and look the other way.'

Melody shot him a dismissive glance. 'Look wherever you like,' she said. 'I'm always well prepared.'

Taking out a large, full-length white towelling robe, she dropped it snugly over her shoulders, giving herself immediately privacy, and in a few seconds had slipped out of her dress and underwear. Then she stepped out of the robe and stood in front of him, her simple black designer costume exhibiting her slender curves and the flat plane of her stomach.

Adam had not taken his eyes off her during this rapid operation, and now, with his mouth drying slightly at the delicious sight of her, he jumped to his feet, released the belt of his trousers and dropped them to the ground, revealing his tight-fitting black swimming trunks—which he'd obviously changed into before they'd left. Then he moved over to her side and took her hand in his.

'Come on,' he said lightly, 'let's make a run for it.'

Caught up in the blissfully relaxing atmosphere of the day, Melody felt her heart soar as they sprinted together across the soft sand. But when they reached the shingle, and then the hard ridge of pebbles at the edge of the water, she was forced to let go of him and raise both arms to steady her balance as they splashed into the waves.

For the next hour they swam and splashed about in the water like schoolchildren. Adam was obviously a much stronger swimmer than Melody, and once or twice he left her to strike out alone. She watched him moving easily through the deep—his over-arm strokes rhythmically purposeful—until she was afraid she was going to lose sight of him altogether. But then he turned and came back to tread water by her side.

'I never like going too far out of my depth,' she confessed, and he grinned at her, his hair plastered to the side of his streaming head and neck.

'A very wise maxim—in all matters,' he said enigmatically.

Presently—reluctantly—they decided to return to dry land. Melody couldn't help hobbling as they reached the pebbles, grimacing as the fine shingle crept between her toes. 'Ouch!' she said, glancing up at Adam. 'This hurts!'

He didn't seem to feel it at all, and swiftly caught her around the waist, half-lifting her towards the sand. And as their soaking bodies made contact Melody felt the hard vigour of his muscular frame close in on her. She gasped, pulling free. Then, to cover her fleeting confusion, she tossed back her dripping ponytail and, laughing, ran ahead of him towards the spot where they'd left their things. But he caught up with her easily and, grasping her arm almost roughly, pulled her along behind him until they flung themselves down on the sand.

'That was fantastic!' Melody panted, collapsing with her arms above her head. 'The last time I bathed in the sea must be about three years ago.' She turned to look at him as he lay prone beside her. 'You're a very strong swimmer, Adam.'

'Oh, I learned even before I could read properly,' he replied. 'And I've had plenty of opportunity to practise since.'

He returned her gaze, wishing with all his heart that he was free—properly free from the emotional shackles he'd cursed himself with. But once he'd made up his mind about something he seldom wavered. He just wished that his mind would leave his body alone.

Sitting up quickly, and grabbing a towel from his rucksack, he started rubbing himself down briskly. 'D'you have any family, Mel? Any brothers or sisters?' he asked casually.

Melody sat up and began drying herself, drawing the towel carefully over her arms and chest so as not to let the sand on her body irritate her skin too much. 'No,' she said slowly. 'There was only ever me and my mother. She died just as I was graduating.' She paused. 'And I never knew my father—well, I can't remember him, anyway,' she amended quickly. 'And, regrettably, I never had siblings.' She stopped what she was doing for a second. 'I've always thought it must be wonderful to have a sister, or a brother—or both!' she added, smiling.

Adam grunted. 'Well, don't they say that what you've never had you'll never miss?' he said shortly, and Melody darted a quick glance at him, noting the sudden darkening of his features and the cynical ring in his tone. She remembered Fee's brief allusion to Adam's brother.

She cleared her throat. 'What about you?' she asked lightly. 'I know that you're lucky enough to still have both your parents living…but do you have any other family?'

'Yes. One brother,' he replied flatly. 'My twin—Rupert.'

Melody feigned surprise. 'Oh—how wonderful! And are you identical?' she asked, wondering if it was possible for there to be someone else who had all Adam's physical attributes.

'No. We are not identical—in any respect.'

In the unusual prolonged silence that followed, Melody was dying to push the conversation on and find out what the 'bad blood' Fee had mentioned was all about. But something made her hesitate. It must obviously be something pretty drastic, she thought. And something he was not going to volunteer to enlighten her about. But she just could not leave it there! She had to find out what had made Adam's mouth become set in a hard, forbidding line.

'And does—Rupert—work for the family firm as well?' she enquired, busying herself with flipping the sand out from between her toes. 'Do you see each other often?'

'No. On both counts,' Adam said curtly. 'A couple of years ago he decided to break away from the rest of us and do his own thing. He and I haven't spoken since. And before you ask, no, I don't miss him, and I'm never likely to.'

There was a long pause after that, then Melody said softly, 'I think that's terribly sad.'

He turned on her then, and said savagely, 'There are many sad things in life. Some of which can't be helped, and some of which should never have been allowed to happen.'

Of course Melody had realised that there must have been some disagreement between the brothers, but still, she thought, civilised people could surely come to terms with it eventually?

'I personally think that if you're lucky enough to have family you should value it,' she said simply. 'I would have loved, *loved*, to have had close relatives.'

'Oh, don't be too upset about being an only child,' he went on brusquely. 'For relationships to work in a family—or anywhere, for that matter—there must be trust, understanding and unselfish love.' He flung his towel down on the sand. 'Believe me, families can be a mixed blessing. They're overrated—well, that's my opinion, anyway. That may sound harsh, but…'

She turned to face him squarely. 'It not only sounds harsh, Adam, it *is* harsh,' she said, trying to keep a trace of bitterness out of her voice. 'I'm sorry that it clearly didn't work for you, but to have someone as close as a brother or sister…to share everything with in bad times as well as good…must be so comforting. Surely there can be no one else that you would feel as close to…no other human bond?' She swallowed a lump in her throat. 'Because blood is the precious thing that unites you…blood is the *lifeline*.'

Adam snorted derisively as he stared back at her. 'Oh, don't you think I know all that?' he said. 'And wouldn't it be amazing if everyone in the world was able to feel close to their "nearest and dearest"?' He spat out the words angrily.

'I've always thought it would be great to have someone to share things with,' Melody went on slowly, but he cut in before she could go on.

'Ah, yes—sharing,' he said, looking away. 'A wonderful concept. If it works.' He stood up suddenly. 'But, hey—why are we spoiling a brilliant afternoon? All this introspection is depressing me!' He reached down and pulled Melody to her feet. 'Let's get dressed and find somewhere for a meal—those sandwiches we ate earlier have become a distant memory, and I'm always hungry after a swim.'

Melody did as she was told, and with the aid of her bathrobe dressed easily, then rubbed at her hair furiously. She knew it would take some time to dry, but the sun, still hot and golden on their backs, would help. Fishing in her bag for her hairbrush, she started to drag it through the unwilling tangles, and glanced up to see Adam watching her.

'That looks like agony,' he commented.

'It is,' she agreed. 'And it also makes my arms ache.'

'Here. Let me.'

He moved over to her side and took the brush from her, and

even though she'd rather have done it herself she didn't object, but stood perfectly still as he deftly worked his way through her long tresses, dragging the brush in long, sweeping strokes from the crown of her head to where the hair ended at her waist. Occasionally he stopped to run his fingers through it gently—which had an almost dizzying effect on Melody, making her nerve-ends tingle from the back of her neck to the top of her thighs. He didn't say anything at all while he was engaged in this operation, seeming to be lost in his own thoughts.

Melody was certainly lost in hers! But then, she thought, she'd always loved someone combing and brushing her hair…it relaxed her, made her feel good. And doing this for her seemed to bring Adam back to normal. When they'd talked about families just now she'd seen a different side to him. Clearly there must have been huge sibling rivalry between the two brothers. She shrugged inwardly. Well, if he was the jealous type it was no concern of hers. Perhaps Rupert had always been the favourite with their parents? It could happen; she knew that. But to bear grudges or to show resentment was un-attractive in a man, as were all the things he'd said about family life. He clearly had no time for relationships in general, she thought, remembering the flippant way he'd answered her when she'd asked if he was married. *No, thanks,* had been his terse reply! But none of this should come as a surprise, she thought. He wanted to be foot-loose and fancy-free, while clearly enjoying the company of women. Winner takes all, in his case!

By the time they left the beach it was nearly seven o'clock. 'There used to be a good place to eat a mile or so further on from here,' Adam said, as he stowed their things into the car boot. 'I haven't been there for ages, and it's probably changed a bit by now—but it may be worth a try.'

They got into the car and drove away. Suddenly beginning to feel deliciously tired and tingly, Melody leaned her head back against the seat. 'That was a most unexpected treat,' she said. She turned to glance at him. 'Many thanks for that, Adam.'

'My pleasure,' he said casually.

'I suppose when one has children beach holidays are a must,' Melody went on. 'We all usually go skiing, or on other activity breaks…'

'Who's "we"?' Adam asked, without looking at her.

'Oh—my friends…workmates,' she replied. 'We don't do very much socialising during the year, but an annual expedition based on healthy exercise seems to have become the norm over recent years.'

He turned to look at her then. 'Well, you're going to miss all that, then—coming down here instead,' he said pointedly.

'Oh, I shan't be let off that lightly,' Melody said. 'I'll have to fit it all in somehow.'

'Mmm…trying to please yourself and everyone else as well can be a pressure,' he said casually. 'I can see that eventually you'll end up letting the cottage to strangers, just to justify your financial outlay and keep the place ticking over,' he went on. 'Empty places soon deteriorate.'

'Oh, I shan't *ever* use it for letting purposes!' Melody declared. 'That was never my thought when I bought it. No…I intended it, and still do, as an escape—a chance for a complete change. Somewhere for me to—what's that current phrase?— "recharge my batteries" from time to time. As often as I can possibly arrange it,' she added.

'Yes, it's a popular concept,' he agreed. 'But for it to work, it must be properly planned.' He paused. 'I don't think you've *really* thought this one out, Mel,' he said, in what to her sounded like a headmaster's admonition! 'It's extremely hard for a life to work on two levels, and to be honest I shouldn't be surprised to see Gatehouse Cottage back on the market in a couple of years from now.'

Melody was stung by that thought. 'It certainly will not be!' she said. What did *he* know of her plans, of her intentions. But, annoyingly, there was a grain of truth in his remarks—not about the possibility of selling, but about her finding it difficult to pack up and come down here for flying visits, glorious as that prospect had seemed when she'd bid for the cottage. Well, she'd prove him wrong! Somehow she'd squeeze enough time out of her frantically busy career to make the trip at least every couple of months. She was not going to be defeated now—and certainly not by the remarks and opinions of this man who was little more than a stranger. Even though he didn't *feel* like a stranger!

Angrily, she turned to look out of the window. She was going to make damned sure that Gatehouse Cottage was hers for a very long time to come. She'd never give him the satisfaction of being proved right!

They reached the restaurant, and Adam clicked his tongue. 'So—it *is* here,' he said, 'but somewhat changed, I fear.'

The place had obviously been taken over by one of the large chains, and, pulling into the huge car park, he glanced across at her. 'Do we risk this—or find somewhere quieter?' he asked.

'This'll be fine by me,' Melody replied coolly, realising that by now she was feeling very hungry.

Inside, the restaurant was heaving with families, and small children's voices were raised piercingly above the general loud conversation and clattering of dishes. Adam looked down at Melody as they entered.

'Do we advance or retreat?' he asked.

'Don't be pathetic,' Melody replied. 'This'll be fine. Look—there's a table for two, right over there in the corner.'

They sat down, and Adam looked around him, his lip curling slightly. 'Ye gods,' he said. 'It's like a zoo. Look over there—there are seven kids in that family!'

Melody couldn't help smiling. 'Seven does seem extravagant,' she said. Then, 'So—you don't like children?'

'Don't know them—so can't express an opinion,' he replied. 'But, as I'm most unlikely to ever have any of my own, the matter is irrelevant.' He paused. 'What about you? Your well-expressed opinion about families leads me to think that you'll probably have a litter of your own one day.'

Melody shrugged. 'It isn't something I've given a lot of thought to,' she said slowly. 'I suppose we would have started a family at some point…but since Crispin died… Well, anyway, I don't somehow think that it's likely now.'

He tilted his head and raised one eyebrow, encouraging her to go on, but Melody decided that enough was enough, and the subject was dropped.

Against their expectations, the service was quick and the food good. Adam chose a rare steak for his meal, while Melody preferred tender lamb cutlets, and, despite the bedlam going on all around them, they both ate heartily.

'See?' she said. 'Despite the prevailing atmosphere, it didn't put us off our supper, did it?

'I told you that swimming always makes me hungry,' Adam said, draining his glass of red wine.

'Yes—and it must have had the same effect on me,' Melody said, putting down her knife and fork.

She glanced up at him for a moment and he held her gaze. She knew that he had been watching her as she ate. She'd have loved to be able to read his mind…or maybe she wouldn't! Because when he looked at her like that she knew very well what would be uppermost in his thoughts. She admitted to herself that it warmed her, made her feel special. But she didn't need this, she reminded herself. She couldn't cope with it! Her plans, whatever his opinion of her, did not include him—or any other member of the male sex!

She picked up her glass of water. 'I am going to pay for this meal, Adam,' she began firmly, determined to assert the fact that she was her own woman, and didn't expect any favours.

'Over my dead body,' he said pleasantly.

'Then we'll fight over it, and I'll make a scene,' she countered.

'Go ahead. No one'll hear you over this din,' he said. Then, 'It'll be a privilege to pay for a beautiful woman to…recharge her batteries. I've certainly recharged my own,' he added. 'That was a good steak.' He reached for his wallet and glanced across at her. 'How about making a start on those trees tomorrow?' he asked casually.

Melody looked back at him steadily. 'Your holiday is being completely swallowed up on my behalf,' she said. 'You really don't need to spend any more time on me, or Gatehouse Cottage. I already feel guilty about all that cleaning you helped me with.'

He shrugged. 'I told you, it's been a pleasant diversion for me,' he said, thinking that if she did prefer to be by herself he'd better back off. Better for both of them—especially him! He was enjoying this woman's company far too much, when all he'd really wanted to do was find out about her and her future intentions for the cottage. Maybe, by some unimagined quirk of circumstance, he might still be able to undermine her decision and get her to sell it on again. Though he didn't feel too optimistic that that would ever happen.

'I think I'll leave the trees until next weekend,' Melody said lightly. 'As a matter of fact I've invited some friends down for a few days—I've said I'll book some rooms for them, and I'm sure they'll enjoy helping out in the garden.'

'What friends are those?'

'Oh—my special mates, Eve and Jon. We work together most of the time.' She paused. 'And they're bringing Jason with them—who I haven't known for quite as long, but…'

'Boyfriend?' Adam asked bluntly.

She gave him a measured glance. 'Sort of. He's working pretty hard at it,' she said. 'He's a nice bloke, actually…I like him.' She reached into her bag for a tissue, thinking of Jason's shock of fair hair and his ready wit. She'd asked Eve to bring him down as well, so that Adam would get the message and maybe make himself scarce for a change. But in doing so she hoped that Jason would not get the wrong idea and see it as encouragement. Because she had no emotional interest in him, and never would have.

The waitress came across then, with their bill. Just as Adam was about to scrutinise it, his mobile rang, and he reached into his pocket to answer it. When Melody saw his expression change, she immediately leaned forward.

'What is it?' she asked quietly.

He shook his head briefly, still listening intently. Then, 'Of course…we'll come straight back—take us about an hour, Callum. And don't worry. We'll sort everything.'

Melody held her breath. 'What *is* it?' she asked again.

Adam stood up quickly. 'It's Fee. She's been taken ill. They're waiting for the ambulance now.'

## CHAPTER SEVEN

THEY couldn't get out of the restaurant fast enough, and in a few moments were sweeping out of the car park, with Adam's foot hard on the accelerator.

Sitting forward in her seat, but staring straight ahead, Melody said, 'What exactly did Callum say, Adam? When did this happen?'

'A couple of hours ago,' he said. 'Apparently Callum had been out walking the dogs, then stopped to spend a few minutes in his workshop at the back—sorting out some wood he's bought. When he went inside he found Fee had collapsed on the stairs.'

Melody was horrified, and turned to look at Adam as he spoke, noting the grim set of his jaw and realising again how close he must be to the pair. He might not have much time for his own kith and kin, she thought fleetingly, but there was no doubt about his loyalty to his friends.

'So, what did the doctor have to say?' Melody asked.

'Not much—except that she should go to hospital immediately.' He paused and glanced across. 'Fee is pregnant, by the way,' he said shortly. 'They're both longing for a family—have been for a long time. But they've already had so many disappointments.' He shook his head briefly. 'This doesn't look good—and Callum sounded desperate with worry.'

Melody looked away, not volunteering the fact that she'd been let in on the hopeful news. 'Poor Fee,' she murmured. Then, 'Why is it that those who really, really, want children sometimes seem to have so much difficulty?'

Adam shrugged. 'They both had the feeling that this time was going to be the lucky one,' he said. 'But it seems to be following a pattern, I'm afraid.' He waited before going on. 'They only told me about it last night in the pub, and they were so upbeat and excited.' He banged his fist on the steering wheel. 'It's so damned unfair!'

'But Callum didn't say that Fee had actually miscarried, did he?' Melody asked. 'She has been feeling the heat all day—we know that. Maybe it's just a faint, a bad turn…?'

'No, it's more than that,' Adam said. 'Apparently she'd been lying there for ages, quite unable to get herself up… And I believe there were other symptoms…' He didn't go on, and Melody bit her lip. She knew that Fee was at a very delicate point in her pregnancy and that anything untoward would be viewed very seriously.

'On a practical level,' Adam said, glancing across at her, 'Poplars is going to be unmanned until Callum returns from the hospital later. That's why he's asked me to get back as soon as possible.'

'Well, what normally happens in an emergency?' Melody asked. 'Don't they have back-up? People in the village…?'

'There are one or two they can usually call on,' he replied. 'But there's this wretched summer flu going around like wildfire, and even the permanent girl who helps with the cleaning has been off for the last two days. It'll be hard to find anyone available. Anyway,' he said, pausing briefly as they approached a crossroads, 'I've told Callum we're on our way. He's going to follow the ambulance and stay with Fee until her condition becomes clearer, though the doctor hinted that she's likely to be kept in for a few days. I told Callum I'd see to the dogs—and everything else—until he gets back.'

Melody sat back in her seat, picturing Fee's attractive features—which must now be twisted with anxiety and desperation. Poor girl, she thought. She wanted to have children so badly. Then Melody's expression cleared slightly. Surely they shouldn't be too pessimistic just yet? she thought. As far as anyone knew, Fee's baby was still where it should be—this could easily be a horrible false alarm, something that could be sorted. Antenatal care had improved dramatically over the years, and women seemed to be giving birth against all the odds. Just thinking along those lines made Melody's heart lift. She somehow couldn't help believing that one day Poplars would ring with the chatter of small voices—and Callum and Fee would be the best parents in the whole world.

It took a bit longer to get back to Poplars than Adam had thought, and it was almost dark when they eventually arrived. Callum's car was nowhere to be seen.

'They've obviously gone,' Adam noted briefly. 'Callum said he'd leave me a message about anything I need to be aware of.'

Melody felt relieved that Fee was already in professional hands and on her way to hospital. The sooner Fee was assessed, and possible treatment begun, the greater the chance of saving her baby, she reasoned.

She followed Adam into the immaculately tidy kitchen, where the dogs—obviously having had their meal for the day—lay comfortably sprawled out on the floor. A hastily scribbled note lay on the table, and Adam picked it up, reading it out loud.

"'Adam—I'm just off. It's nine-twenty. Fee has already gone in the ambulance. I hope to be back before morning, but could you hold the fort until then? You know how everything ticks. Fee is comfy at the moment. Thanks, mate. C.'"

As Adam looked down at her, Melody saw a look of deep

concern on the handsome features, and she touched his hand gently. 'Don't worry too much,' she said, trying to sound more optimistic than she felt. 'This doesn't have to have a bad ending, and Fee is in the best hands,' she added.

'Yes, I know that,' he said, bending to smooth the glossy heads of the animals, who'd ambled over to his side. 'But Callum sounded so desperate on the phone. I really wonder whether they can tolerate yet another disappointment. I mean, how much more of this can they take?' He stood back and ran his hand through his hair. 'They're good, kind, hard-working people…they don't deserve this trauma every time!'

Melody looked around her. 'What happens if Callum has to stay with Fee and doesn't get back tomorrow?' she asked.

'Well, I'll have to explain to the guests—all the rooms are occupied, so we have a full house—and tell them that cooked breakfasts are off the menu. They'll just have to be satisfied with cold stuff.' He paused. 'Do you know, if I *do* have to tell them that it'll be a first for Poplars? In all the years that Callum and Fee have run the place they've kept it going without a hitch—even when Fee was going through a bad patch.' He bit his lip. 'I know they just hate any disruption, or any reason for their guests to be dissatisfied.'

'Well, then,' Melody said, a rising note of determination in her voice. 'We'll make sure that doesn't happen.' She looked up at him. 'As long as every guest doesn't turn up at exactly the same moment for their breakfast in the morning, I can cope with grilling bacon and frying eggs, and—'

He looked down into her upturned face and instinctively cupped his hand under her chin. 'Are you saying…? Do you mean that you'd be prepared to help out?' he asked uncertainly.

She closed her hand over his wrist briefly. 'Adam,' she said patiently. 'I was trained from a very early age how to rise to any occasion.' She turned away. 'You know this place as well as anyone. Show me where they keep everything, and tomorrow—if it turns out to be necessary—I cook, you serve!' A faint smile played on her lips as she imagined Adam waiting at table, with a fresh white teatowel draped over his arm, maybe having to be polite to an unreasonable guest! Well, she'd make sure she gave no one any reason to complain, she thought firmly. She'd get up really early—give herself time to get to grips with any peculiarities in Fee's cooking equipment.

'You're finding something funny?' he asked, noting her amused expression but looking relieved that, between them, they might save the situation.

She hastily corrected him. 'No,' she said flatly. 'Of course not. I was just thinking what a strange turn my holiday seems to be taking. Ten days ago I had no idea that anything out of the ordinary was going to happen. I'd even thought I might go back to London sooner rather than later…but of course that was before I saw the sign outside Gatehouse Cottage.' *And before I met you,* she could have added, but didn't.

Adam went over to study the large boldly printed chart on the back of the door, running his finger along the columns. 'Good,' he said, 'no one appears to want early breakfast tomorrow, and with a bit of luck there shouldn't be any undue bottlenecks. Oh…the lady in room seven is allergic to wheat, so she has to have special bread, which is apparently in a sealed bag in the cabinet. "Not to be in contact with other bread", it says here,' he added. He continued perusing the chart, then, 'And the guests in room two are checking out tomorrow. Their bill is already worked out, apparently, with all details in the safe.' He turned around and looked over to Melody. 'D'you think we're up to this, Mel? Up to the challenge?' he asked, only half joking.

She looked back at him eagerly. 'I don't *think* so, I *know* so,' she replied, glancing up at the big clock on the wall. 'But—

first things first—I'd better go to bed, stock up on my energy reserves for the morning!'

'Good thinking,' he said. 'When I've locked up at midnight I'll hit the sack, too. But the dogs will need their last walk in a few minutes.'

Melody picked up her holdall from the chair and went to open the door, turning briefly. 'By the way—thanks again for taking me to the seaside,' she said. 'It's been a…a good day….'

He grinned down at her. 'Even if it has ended rather unexpectedly,' he said. Then his expression clouded. 'I hope they've stabilised Fee,' he said. 'If she does lose this baby, I don't know what words we can use to comfort her.'

'Well, as far as we know, the worst has not happened,' Melody said firmly. 'And the best thing we can do is to keep the wheels turning here and put their minds at rest on that score, at least.' She stifled a yawn, leaning against the wall for a second. 'But if I don't lie down soon, I'll fall down! I'm starting to ache in every limb since that swim!'

Adam opened the door for her at once, and as she brushed past him he held her arm gently for a moment.

'Callum is sure to ring me. To let me know how things are,' he said, 'and also when he's likely to be coming back.' He hesitated. 'I won't disturb you to tell you, but I'll slip a note under your door—for you to see when you wake in the morning.'

'I'll set my alarm to go off early,' Melody said, yawning properly this time.

Adam moved away from her, then had a sudden thought. 'Would you like a cup of tea?' he asked. 'Or something stronger?'

She glanced up at him quickly. 'How did you guess? A cup of tea would be fantastic,' she said. 'No sugar, and just a dash of milk, thanks.'

'I'll bring it up in a few minutes,' he said, adding, 'You do look all-in, Mel.'

Upstairs, Melody spent as few minutes as possible in the bathroom, then set her travel alarm clock for half past six before sinking down onto the bed gratefully, not even bothering to get beneath the duvet. This had been one long day, she thought. Brilliant in many ways—too many ways!—but ending unthinkably with Fee being rushed off like that. Even in her near sleeping state, Melody frowned in sympathy. The signs were not good, she realised, despite her forced optimism when she and Adam had been discussing it.

Adam…. In her mind's eye, she saw how the seawater had glistened and run down his body as they'd walked across the sand, the muscles in his suntanned thighs rippling and tightening as he'd held her closely, supporting her over the pebbles. With sleep now almost upon her, Melody shifted slightly on the bed. This had to stop, she thought. It *must* stop! She seemed to have been thrust into a whirlpool since the moment she'd purchased Gatehouse Cottage. The property seemed to have come complete with a resident male who just happened to be tall, dark, handsome—and horribly desirable! Desire? *Desire?* That had become a defunct word in her life—or she'd thought so! Go away—go *away*! she implored whoever was listening. Don't want it, don't need it… Her eyes flickered open for a second. 'That's not true,' she whispered to herself. 'The truth is—I'm *frightened* of it!' Then, utterly exhausted, sleep finally claimed her.

Presently there came a discreet tap on her door, and Adam's low voice saying her name. He failed to rouse her, and he turned the handle gently and went inside, closing the door behind him.

Going over to the bed, he looked down on Melody's inert form, saw her slender body barely covered by the simple nightdress she was wearing. She'd released her ponytail so that her hair was spread out in a luxurious fan of honey-coloured waves across the pillow, and her eyelashes, resting gently on the curve of her cheek, must be the longest he'd ever seen on a woman.

He swallowed, putting the mug of tea down quietly on the bedside table. The picture she presented had sent his senses rocketing, and he turned away. His natural instinct was to slip in alongside her—hold her, caress her… But he knew he'd be wasting his time. Not because she was frigid—she was far from that; she was warm and utterly appealing, in a certain way irresistible! But she was definitely not the sort of woman to engage in temporary relationships—there'd be no such thing as a quick fling in *her* life! And anyway, he thought, irritated again at the way his mind was working, he had no wish—or intention—to ever commit himself again to anything permanent. So he might as well accept this no-win situation and take the whole business of this woman crossing his path at face value. And stop allowing his thoughts to give him all this aggro!

Melody woke even before the alarm went off. She'd slept well, and now, feeling refreshed and ready for anything the day might bring, she slid out of bed and went over to the door. A note lay on the floor, and she picked it up, going over to the window-sill and pulling the curtains aside. A ray of sunlight shafted across Adam's strong, purposeful writing on the paper.

One a.m. It looks like action stations, Mel. Callum was advised to stay with Fee for the moment—at least until they've seen the consultant together, which they hope will be today. I've told him we're taking over until he gets back, and he's over the moon about that. But the best news is that Fee hasn't lost the baby—yet. See you later!

Melody's heart lifted—all was not lost! she thought. The worst had not happened. And, meanwhile, there was a guesthouse to run!

She showered and pulled on fresh jeans and a white T-shirt, dragging her hair back in a formal knot on top, to keep it well out of the way. Then, going quickly downstairs, she met Adam at the kitchen door as he came in with the dogs.

'You've had a good rest,' he said approvingly, noting her bright eyes and wide-awake manner.

'Slept like a log,' she replied. 'Thank you for the tea, by the way,' she added, not bothering to admit that she'd not tasted it because she hadn't seen it until she woke up.

'You didn't answer my knock so I just left it,' he said.

'Yes, thanks,' she murmured, hoping that she hadn't been exposing too much of herself at the time… Well, not enough to interest his perceptive gaze, she thought. But she didn't really care one way or the other.

In the kitchen, the dogs immediately went over to their water bowls and lapped furiously. 'I've already checked the dining room,' Adam said. 'All the tables are set for breakfast, and all we have to do at the moment is put the cereals out—they're stacked in the tall cupboard over there. The juices and fruits are obviously in the fridge—to go in those glass bowls on the shelf.' He paused. 'Everyone helps themselves to all that, of course…' he added.

'Yes. That's the easy bit,' Melody said. 'Now, let's see if I can get the bacon just as everyone wants it—and fry the eggs without damaging the yolks!'

Adam put the kettle on, looking across at her. 'I think the cook should be fed first,' he said. 'Tea and toast do you, Mel?'

'Perfect,' she said, adding, 'And I can always cook for you later on, if you like…'

'Oh, I seldom eat fried breakfasts,' Adam said, reaching for two mugs for their tea. 'But you never know—I might be tempted.'

They smiled across at each other as the kettle began to hum, and Melody felt a ridiculous sense of anticipation. She'd never been in the catering business before—this was going to be a whole new experience! But her greatest sense was one of genuine pleasure in helping out Adam's friends—to at least do something to minimise their present crisis. Because, although she tried hard to push it from her mind, she could not stop feeling guilty about the purchase of the cottage—the cottage they had wanted so badly. For her, it had been an unbelievable bolt from the blue, and somehow it didn't seem quite fair that it was hers.

Together, they did everything they could before the guests started arriving for breakfast, and soon the delicious aroma of percolating coffee—which Adam took charge of—seemed to bring several of them down at once. By half past eight, Melody had grilled a couple of dozen sausages, large numbers of delectable rashers of back bacon—all put aside to keep warm—while lining up dishes of mushrooms and slices of black pudding ready to be fried. The boxes of eggs stood on the kitchen table, to be done last. Turning briefly from her task, she wiped her brow with the back of her hand. Even this early, the sun was hot as it streamed through the open window.

Adam came in from the dining room to fetch more milk, pouring it into a huge glass jug. 'So far, so good,' he said. 'They're all munching away on their cereals at the moment.'

'How many full English breakfasts did you say you'd be needing?' Melody asked, not looking at him as she lifted hot slices of fried bread from the pan.

'Six—almost due,' he said. 'When you're ready, Mel.'

'Just the eggs, then,' Melody said, turning to crack them open. 'Fingers crossed that the yolks don't break and I can present them just like Fee does,' she said, glancing up at him.

He touched her shoulder briefly. 'You're doing Fee proud,' he said—and meant it. Because Melody had entered willingly into the whole episode—in the middle of her holiday, after all, he reminded himself. He'd observed the precise way she'd organised all the food, her deft handling of Fee's pans and utensils. She was certainly no slouch, he thought, fascinated to see how her small hands slid the eggs into the hot fat, with not a single one broken in the process. Well, she'd informed him that she could rise to any occasion, and now she was proving it!

'I'll clear away the dirty dishes,' he said over his shoulder as he went out, 'and then come back for the breakfasts. If you're sure you're ready?' he added.

'I'm ready,' Melody said, lining up warm plates in a row, and placing all the items of cooked food onto them. 'One without black pudding, and three with double eggs,' she chanted aloud. 'One without black pudding, and three with double eggs…' She kept repeating the mantra, hoping that she'd got it the right way around, and added the slices of fried bread that everyone had asked for. Then she carefully wiped the edges of the plates with a clean teatowel, and stood back. They looked good, she congratulated herself.

Adam came back almost at once, and immediately started to load the dishwasher. 'Four more have just come down,' he said. 'Two want full English, one without sausage. And one wants scrambled eggs, and one poached. Those last two on toast, please, one of which must be gluten-free.'

'Okay—that special bread is over there,' Melody said. 'I'll remember.'

Adam loaded two large trays with the food already prepared, and looked at Melody. 'This all looks fantastic, Mel,' he said. 'You're doing a great job!'

'You, too,' she replied, looking up at him, her face flushed from the heat of the cooker.

At nine-thirty, the last guest arrived for his breakfast. By now the dining room was almost deserted, and Melody couldn't help feeling relieved that the end was in sight. She plonked herself down on one of the kitchen chairs for a moment, staring at the hard-worked toaster in front of her. She'd lost count of the number of slices she'd sent into the dining room, and was thinking that if none of the guests had another crumb to eat that day they'd hardly starve! But everyone had been very co-operative and pleasant when Adam had briefly explained that the owners had been called away unexpectedly.

'Well, we've got nothing to complain about,' someone said. 'The owners are lucky to have such efficient stand-ins!'

In a few moments Adam came back in, looking slightly rueful. 'Sorry, Mel—our last guest has requested poached eggs on haddock. He's chomping away on a big bowl of muesli at the moment…'

'Where's the haddock?' Melody asked anxiously. 'I haven't seen any, or given fish a thought. It's certainly not in the fridge—I know everything that's there off by heart…'

'Try the freezer, then,' Adam said. 'It must be in there.'

It was, and it was frozen solid. Muttering under her breath, cross that she hadn't spotted it on the menu, Melody split open the pack and put a fillet into the microwave to defrost. Then she filled the kettle for boiling water.

'This is going to take a few minutes,' she said, looking up at Adam. 'Go and keep him talking—or give him some more cereal!'

Adam grinned at her as he left the room, while Melody concentrated on the job in hand. Why couldn't this guest have asked for bacon and eggs, like everyone else? she thought. But presently, with the fillet of sunshine-yellow haddock and two perfectly poached eggs sitting proudly on top, she felt quite pleased with herself. Well, if she was asked for that again she'd be ready, she thought.

Eventually, fully satisfied, the man left the dining room. Adam and Melody immediately cleared the tables, setting them all again with crockery and cutlery for the following day, and presently, in the kitchen, with the fully laden dishwasher gurgling and gushing away in the corner, Adam sat astride one of the chairs, draping his arms over the back of it in mock fatigue.

'Blimey,' he said quietly. 'That was all go. Well done, Mel. You did a fantastic job.'

'It was a joint effort,' she acknowledged, sitting down as well, and leaning her arms on the table. 'And once I got into the swing of it I rather enjoyed myself,' she said. 'I might even consider a new career!' She paused. 'How much help does Fee have normally?' she asked.

'Only one part-time girl for breakfasts,' he replied. 'But Callum's always on hand. And don't forget they've been doing this a long time. They're experienced. We're not!'

After a few minutes Melody stood up and began clearing everything away, replacing the pots and pans she'd used back in their rightful place. Adam still sat, watching her. 'I have an imminent appointment with my shower,' she said, 'and I may be gone some time!'

He waited before answering. Then, 'Why don't you leave that until later…when we've finished?'

Melody frowned. 'But we have, haven't we?' she said.

'We've fed everyone, certainly,' he agreed. 'But as soon as they've all disappeared for the day there are the rooms to service…'

Melody clapped her hand over her mouth. 'Oh, what an *idiot*! I haven't given the rooms a single thought.' She paused. 'Is no one coming in to help?'

'Unlikely,' Adam said casually. 'I had another call from Callum early this morning—no change in Fee, by the way—and he said that the girl who usually helps with the rooms is still not well enough… She'll turn up if she feels like it, apparently. But I don't think we should count on it. Anyway,' he added, 'we've got all day. It's not as if we have to provide evening meals as well!'

Melody sat back down on her chair for a second, then immediately got up again. 'Right. Well, then. Come on,' she said, looking across at him. 'Where do we begin?'

'There's a trolley in the utility room always set up with everything necessary,' Adam said, getting up as well.

Just then there was a discreet tap on the door. The guests who were leaving wanted to settle their bill, and Adam ushered them over to the desk in the hall, making pleasantries as he went. In the kitchen, Melody looked around her. Well, everything was neat and tidy here, she thought. Now for the next stage in the proceedings!

As Adam was finally wishing the departing guests a safe journey onwards, he heard a short, sharp scream, and Melody's voice ringing out.

'Oh…damn you—*damn* you!' he heard. 'You swine!'

'*What* the—?' he said under his breath, and he burst open the kitchen door, seeing Melody over by the window, rubbing furiously at her arm, clearly very agitated. 'What ever is it?' he demanded, reaching her side in a couple of strides.

'A wasp! It just flew in through the window and pitched on my arm and stung me! The wretched thing!' she cried. 'I did nothing to deserve that…I didn't even see it! Not until I felt it!' She kept rubbing. 'I *hate* wasps! What are they *for*, anyway? What purpose do they serve?'

Although slightly concerned, Adam made himself keep a straight face as he took her arm and examined it closely. He didn't bother to mention that they often had swarms of the things at this time of year—or that when the fruit-picking began down at her cottage she was likely to encounter one or two more!

'I can see the sting,' he murmured. 'Hold still a minute.' Then he took her arm to his mouth and sucked at it firmly.

'Ow—ow!' Melody said pathetically. 'It really hurts! I've only ever been stung once before in my life, and I didn't appreciate it then, either! Wretched spiteful creature!'

For a few moments neither of them spoke, while Adam continued tugging at her skin with his lips and tongue, peering at it every now and then. Then, satisfied, he looked down at Melody. 'It's out now,' he said soothingly. 'Just dab some vinegar on the sore spot—you'll soon be good as new.'

But he didn't let go of her arm. He just brought it once more to his lips…only this time he kissed it—once, twice, three times—gently. With her eyes open, Melody looked up at him. And suddenly, without any warning, their lips met, tentatively at first, then with increasing passion as he wrapped his arms around her, drawing her in close to him as if he never wanted to let her go. To his enormous pleasure and delight, she didn't resist, but entered into it with him…allowed herself to desire…and to be desired.

Melody felt her senses swimming as they stayed locked together in a state of heightened excitement, then she eased herself away—gently but firmly.

'Thank you,' she said shakily. 'For removing the wasp sting, I mean,' she added.

He smiled down, his body painfully taut with his sensual need of her. 'I enjoyed every second of it,' he murmured softly.

For a few moments neither of them said anything in the rather tense atmosphere, then Melody's commonsense took over—and brought her back to earth with a bang! What was going on? she asked herself. Was she in the middle of a dream? A dream in which she'd just cooked breakfast for everyone at the guesthouse that she was *paying* to stay in…and in which, thanks to a wasp sting, she'd just allowed Adam Carlisle to kiss her in the sort of way she'd never expected to experience ever again? Worst of all—she'd wanted him to!

'I'm sorry,' she said, glancing quickly up at him. 'That…that must have been the effect of the wasp stinging me.' She swallowed. 'It…sort of took me by surprise.'

He didn't attempt to touch her again, but let his eyes do the talking…and they were talking volumes! 'Don't apologise,' he said softly. 'I like surprises. Especially ones like that.'

# CHAPTER EIGHT

THE rest of the day passed in a blur of activity as, between them, Adam and Melody went into each of the rooms. Melody automatically took charge of the order in which everything should be done, but it was Adam who knew which cupboards held the fresh linen, where all Fee's equipment was kept, and it was he who insisted on wielding the heavy vacuum cleaner—which he did with ferocious energy—while charging up and down the stairs to answer the phone or fetch something they needed from the ground floor.

'Fee has a thing about disinfecting everything,' Adam said as he reached for a bottle of detergent, and Melody nodded.

During her short stay, she'd been gratefully aware of how spotless her room and bathroom were kept, but today was even more aware that her own mother would have spent years doing what *she* was doing now. And as she'd dusted the windowsills and picture frames she'd had the weirdest sense that Frances was there, too, helping her. Stop imagining things, she scolded herself, more than once. Anyway, Callum and Fee had done so much renovating her mother would have hardly recognised the place. But Melody couldn't avoid the feeling that the very walls seemed to speak of the past, and of the people who'd lived in it. And that had the distinct advantage of making what they were doing actually pleasurable—it became a surprisingly happy chance, rather than a chore. Together with all the cleaning they'd done at the cottage, her holiday was indeed turning into a sort of activity break, but one which not many people would ever sign up for! she thought.

Plunging herself so enthusiastically into what she was doing also provided Melody with an emotional shield against the turmoil that was threatening to engulf her. Because the atmosphere between her and Adam had perceptibly changed—and she knew he felt it, too. Their eyes had barely met since he'd kissed her—yet it was the thing starkly uppermost in her mind. The feeling of his arms wrapped around her so comfortingly, so protectively. Her head against his chest, hearing the thudding of his heart… Then the fusing of their lips, which had caused her emotions to rocket off into outer space, making her knees almost give way.

But along with all the other good things she'd been taught, Melody had more than her fair share of common sense, and she recognised the fleeting passion she was experiencing as just that—fleeting. A holiday infatuation. That was it, she told herself. A pointless, temporary attraction to someone she'd met during a time away when neither of them had the distraction of more important, essential matters. Oh, they'd no doubt promise to keep in touch—he'd ring, she'd ring, they'd meet up, make plans. Except they wouldn't, of course. With the link of sun and summer and relaxation gone, their association would melt away like ice in the sunshine, and that would be that.

And that would suit him very well, thank you, she thought. Where women and sex were concerned, he wore his *modus operandi* for all to see: take what you can, when you can, with no expectations of anything more. He was certainly no chauvinist—she freely admitted that—but he fitted the type of male she'd met many times before. The sort who took what he could get, but didn't expect to part with any more of himself than he wanted to give. And that was fine by her! That was exactly what she wanted—no more ties, no more tears, *ever*. That morning they'd already taken a dangerous step too far, but no harm— no real harm—had been done, and that was how it must stay. And the marked coolness between them now proved to her that those were his sentiments, too.

Just then he ran up the stairs two at a time, after having gone to answer the phone, and Melody said, 'I want everything to look as good as when Fee's here.' She glanced up at him as she sprayed polish on the curved mahogany banister, and rubbed at it briskly.

He shook his head briefly as he coiled up the flex of the vacuum cleaner. 'Well, if you put any more effort into that,' he observed dryly, 'it'll disappear—and so will you. Give yourself a break, Mel. You're not a carthorse.'

That evening Callum returned for a flying visit, and was overwhelmed by how Adam and Melody had been handling everything.

'I can't thank you both enough,' he said, kneeling down on the kitchen floor to make a fuss of the dogs. 'All I can say is that when you're up against it, you really find out who your true friends are.'

Adam shot a quick glance at Melody, and although she'd deliberately tried to avoid making anything that could be described as meaningful eye contact with him since their intimate coupling, he managed to fix his gaze to hers. His conspiratorial wink dented her reserve for a second, then, smiling briefly, she looked away.

'Oh, I've carried out all Mel's commands to the letter,' he said. 'She's a hard task-master! But truthfully, Callum, it's a pleasure to be of some use at a time like this. Don't worry about it.'

'I'll be honest, Adam, knowing that you were here set my mind at rest—not to mention Fee's. We've hardly given a thought to Poplars…'

'I should hope not!' Melody said. 'Now, Callum, tell us the latest…tell us the important bit.'

Callum sat down heavily on one of the comfortable, well-worn chairs and looked up at them. 'Well, as you already know, our baby is still holding his/her own…' he began.

Melody felt a curious pang of something she found hard to explain. The man had referred to 'our' baby—even though the scrap of humanity had such a long way to go before it finally emerged into the world.

'And although we've been this way before,' Callum went on, 'we're pinning our hopes on an eminent specialist who's visiting the hospital tomorrow or the day after—they're not sure which. He's apparently a leading light in this field, and there's a new drug available which might help Fee to go full-term. But we both need to talk to him—so I'll have to go back to the hospital, I'm afraid. And just wait for him to turn up. As always, there are issues which will need to be discussed, and we must both be there.' He made an apologetic face. 'I'm really sorry to take advantage of you like this, but I'm between a rock and a hard place, and—'

'Shut up, Callum,' Adam said. 'You don't need to apologise to *me*, for heaven's sake! About anything!'

'No, I know that.' Callum turned to Melody. 'This guy comes under the heading of "Super Mate",' he said, with a detectable break in his voice. 'Nothing is ever too much for him. He's helped us out so much over the years… I can heartily recommend him—in all respects!'

A cushion came flying across the room and landed squarely on Callum's head as Adam hurled it. 'I repeat—*shut up*,' he said. 'What the hell else are friends for?'

'But you, Mel,' Callum said, turning to her. 'Fee and I can't begin to thank you. We've heard all about how you've stepped so magnificently into the breach…as if you'd been born to it! And I mean you're on *holiday*, for Pete's sake!'

Melody smiled. 'You know, Callum, I've come to the conclusion that I'm not very good at prolonged periods of inactivity,' she said. 'I've already had a good break…pleasing myself, relaxing…and I think Adam might have been feeling the same. He was determined to help me clean my cottage— as if he needed that on *his* holiday!' She paused. 'You just make sure that Fee stays safely where she is until they're satisfied she and the baby are okay.'

'Well, as I said, we're pinning our hopes on this new man and his new drug,' Callum said, getting up from the chair. 'But now what I need is a shower and a fresh change of clothes— and Fee's asked me to take some stuff back for her.' He turned to Adam. 'The room which became vacant today—' he began, and Adam interrupted.

'Is vacant no longer,' he said. 'I could have let it three times over.'

'Great,' Callum said. 'But we're expecting other vacancies before the end of the week, aren't we? If I remember rightly?'

'Then that'll be very convenient,' Melody said. 'Three friends of mine are coming to visit at the weekend, and have asked me to fix them up. They'll love it here.' She didn't look at Adam as she spoke.

'Ah, yes, your friends from the big city,' he said lazily. 'We must take special care that all *their* needs are supplied.'

Now she *did* look at him. The expression on his face was as blank as hers, and told her nothing. But just thinking about Eve and Jon—and Jason—went some way towards helping Melody adjust her thinking. Their presence here would dilute the situation, would help her to shake off the 'Adam effect' and remind her that in the very near future she would be out of here and back to normality. Because she hadn't felt normal since she'd set foot in the area. Hadn't felt normal since she'd parted with all that money and become a two-home owner. And she hadn't felt normal since she'd met Adam Carlisle. She had allowed him to unfasten—so easily, it seemed to her—the protective cloak she'd wrapped around her emotions ever since Crispin had been taken from her.

Two days later, both part-time girls had returned to work—which did lessen the load dramatically, although privately Melody couldn't help thinking that she and Adam had managed more efficiently without them. Then, by arrangement with Callum, they were joined by the mother of one of the girls, who apparently sometimes worked for Fee. Which released Adam and Melody to resume their own plans.

That morning, Melody had driven away early—not even stopping to have breakfast before she went, in order to prevent bumping into Adam—determined to spend time by herself and to explore some of the area new to her. It was true that since Callum's departure they had spent less time together, and it didn't please Melody to realise that she missed Adam's presence—that even in the short time they'd known each other she'd come to depend on his company. This made her even more certain that she should put some space between them.

The following morning, the day before her friends were due to arrive, Melody wandered down Poplars' long drive towards Gatehouse Cottage, realising that she'd barely thought about it over the last few days. Of course at the moment there was nothing for her to do there—other than go inside and admire it all over again, and form mental pictures as to how she was going to furnish it. She'd already decided that the walls were to be washed throughout in a mellow buttermilk shade, with white gloss paint on all the woodwork. That would give her wonderful scope to fill the place with colourful furnishings and bright paintings, she decided.

Opening the front door, she stepped inside, aware again of the sense of awe she felt at owning this modest but desirable dwelling. Because this was not just *any* dwelling—something she might have just stumbled across. She had unwittingly come home—to the home she'd been told about so often that it felt familiar and warmly embracing. She smiled briefly as she looked around her. It smelt and looked clean and sweet and wholesome—thanks to the hard work she and Adam had put in the other day. How long ago that seemed now! she thought. And once the decorators had come and gone—she'd sort that out as soon as she got back to London—the cottage would be ready to welcome her as its new owner.

Despite the rather snide comments Adam had made about her not having the time or opportunity to come down here very often, she'd prove him wrong! She'd mark up her calendar with possible dates, and make sure that nothing prevented her from keeping them!

Going up the narrow staircase, she peeped into the spotless bathroom, and shivered again as she remembered how that spider had dropped down inside her T-shirt, and how she'd screamed like an idiot! And how Adam had rushed to her side and held her close. Standing quite still for a second, she realised that she'd never, ever go inside this room again without remembering the incident…without remembering Adam. Because it had been a turning point in her life. A point at which she'd had to face up to a need she'd thought she'd conquered. And which she'd thought she would never feel again.

Striding across the fields, calling brusquely to the dogs to keep up, Adam's expression was dark. He was annoyed and angry with himself. Despite everything that had happened since, he still couldn't believe that he'd allowed himself to get carried away the other morning and actually kiss Mel...even if it *was* something which had featured in a number of his dreams!

She was proving to be so much more than just a female who'd titillated his male instincts. Seeing the way she'd responded so readily to Callum and Fee's present dilemma had taken him by surprise. Of course he'd already witnessed her enthusiasm for cleaning up her own precious acquisition—but that was different. That was only to be expected. Putting in time and effort on your own behalf was not particularly laudable—anyone would do it. But to be deeply concerned about others—and to be ready to do something about it as she had—was a different matter entirely.

And the embarrassing part of it was he felt she resented the liberty he'd taken. There had been a deliberate coolness in her attitude ever since—as he should have known there would be. She was not a run-of-the-mill woman who'd enjoy a light relationship and treat it for what it was: a pleasurable but temporary phase. He frowned as his thoughts ran on. For a highly desirable woman like her, keeping unwelcome suitors at bay must be an ongoing problem, he thought—especially in the City, full of sharp-suited, superficial men with loaded wallets. Yet, he reminded himself, it couldn't be denied that she'd *enjoyed* their encounter, brief though it had been. For those few precious seconds she'd been his—it was only afterwards that she'd appeared to regret it.

He shrugged. If she was saying thanks, but no thanks, well, he'd comply—for his own good as well as hers. He'd made up his mind that there would not be a woman alive on this earth who'd ever leave him feeling so betrayed again. Because how could he know who to trust? He'd thought Lucy was the woman of his dreams, that they'd have a long and happy life together, hopefully here in the village, among all that he knew and loved. But the unthinkable thing which had happened had been so much more than the break-up of a couple…it had been a shattering, devastating experience, and had touched too many other lives as well as his own.

Bringing all these thoughts to the front of his mind had creased the handsome brow, set the uncompromising mouth in a formidable line. Enough was enough. It was time for him to pack up and go back to work—a long way from all this. Distance had its merits, and he was going to put some between himself and the new owner of Gatehouse Cottage as soon as possible.

The end of his walk had brought him to the back of the cottage, and without really wondering why he was doing it, he went around the front and up the path to look in at the window—and then saw the front door was open. Automatically he pushed it wider and went inside—just as Melody was coming down the stairs.

'Oh…hi,' she said, as she came down to stand in front of him.

'Hi,' he said casually, not bothering to give any explanation as to why he was there—because he had none. Then, 'I've been walking the dogs—saw the door open…'

She smiled briefly. 'I've just been daydreaming,' she said. 'Picturing where I'm going to put everything. After I've bought it all!'

For a second Adam experienced a wave of something approaching dislike of her and all her enthusiasm, remembering all too clearly how she'd breezed in and spoiled the plans of his best friends. And then he stared down at her. She was simply dressed, in a short above-the-knee denim skirt, her feet barely covered in dainty narrow-strapped white sandals, and her white blouse was trimmed with a tiny edging of lace at the neck and cap sleeves. As usual, her hair was shining as golden as a buttercup, held back from her face by a white scrunchie. Adam swallowed, feeling the familiar rush of adrenalin hit him. He cleared his throat.

'I've had a call from Callum. He's due home tonight—and Fee is coming back early next week,' he said.

Melody's eyes lit up. 'Oh—that's fantastic. What have they said about the baby?' she asked, going into the sitting room and turning to face him as he followed her.

'Well…so far, so good. Of course no one's committing themselves, but the specialist seems to think that there's more than a glimmer of hope this time,' he said. 'Fee apparently has a very particular genetic condition that the drug they propose using might overcome. She's been instructed to rest up for the next few weeks.'

Melody clapped her hands in delight. 'Oh, Adam—that… that's really great!' she exclaimed. 'They must both be thrilled…because there *is* real hope, isn't there?'

'It looks like it,' he said guardedly. 'Naturally they're terrified to tempt fate by being too optimistic, too soon. But I could tell by Callum's voice how excited they already are.'

'Well, *I'm* excited, too!' Melody said. 'Just imagine—one of those guest rooms being turned into a nursery!' She paused. 'I know which one I'd choose—the one that looks over that big horse chestnut tree, that gets the sun in the morning.'

'Steady on,' Adam said easily. 'There'll be plenty of time for all that in due course. When Miss or Master Brown puts in an appearance.'

Together they went outside, and the dogs—who'd been lying on the front lawn—got up to greet them. Melody's mobile rang, and she turned away to answer it. Adam crouched down to fondle the dogs, unavoidably hearing what was being said.

'Oh—hello, Jason…' Melody said. 'How's things?' There was a few moments' silence as she listened. Then, 'Oh, dear—no. Oh, what a shame… Well, let's make it another time, then, shall we?

I mean… Sorry? Are you sure you want to do that? Won't it be more…well, fun, when the others are able to come as well?'

There was another silence, and Adam, glancing up at her, saw Melody's expression change.

'Well, of course. If you really think you want to… Yes, I've fixed you a room. I'll just cancel the one I've booked for Eve and Jon.' There was another long pause. 'Well, give them my love—I'll be back in just over a week, in any case. And I'll see you tomorrow night sometime. You've got the directions I sent to Eve? I think you'll find them straightforward enough. Okay…okay. See you tomorrow. Bye… Bye, Jason.'

Melody snapped her phone shut and glanced down at Adam. 'Well, that's a shame,' she said. 'My friends—Eve and Jon—have both gone down with a really bad dose of something horrible, so they won't be coming tomorrow after all.' She sighed. 'But Jason—Jason is driving down by himself.'

'Well—that'll be cosy, won't it?' Adam said laconically. 'Just the two of you. He'll have you all to himself.'

Melody shot him a direct glance—and remembered why she'd invited Jason to come down in the first place! To stop Adam getting to her emotionally and also to send out a message to *him*. But even as she thought about it she wanted to curl up inside. The thought of having to entertain Jason by herself for forty-eight hours wasn't something she was looking forward to. She had tried, as tactfully as possible, to put him off, but he wasn't having any of it. The tables had been neatly turned on her and she was going to have to be an unwilling participant in a game of pretend. She desperately hoped that Jason wasn't coming with the wrong idea…that she had a special reason for inviting him… She groaned inwardly. What had she let herself in for?

# CHAPTER NINE

'CALLUM—I really feel that I should be helping out in the kitchen,' Melody said next morning, as she took her seat in the dining room, glancing up at him as he came towards her.

He grinned, and Melody couldn't help thinking how young and boyish he looked—compared to how he'd appeared the other night. Then he'd seemed so tired and careworn, but this morning it was different—now that he had sound reasons to be optimistic.

'I am so, *so* pleased that Fee is okay—is *going* to be to okay!' she amended. 'It's such good news, Callum.'

'It is—but fingers crossed,' he said carefully. 'For my part, I feel I should be serving *you* smoked salmon and champagne! Fee and I will never be able to thank you enough for all you did while I was with her at the hospital, Mel.'

'Oh, I won't be needing anything like that, thank you.' Melody smiled. 'Just some of your lovely scrambled eggs, please, Callum.' She paused. 'I didn't see you come home last night,' she added. 'Were you very late getting back?'

'No—not too bad. But you'd obviously already gone to bed, Mel.'

'Yes—I was rather tired,' Melody said.

In fact, she had purposely gone to her room early, so as not to give Adam the chance to invite her somewhere for supper. In any case, she'd been to the village during the day and bought a packet of sandwiches from the post office, which she'd had with the cup of tea she'd been able to make with the things available by her bedside.

'Well, Adam and I did sit up for a bit—talking,' Callum said. 'And opened a bottle or two to keep our throats lubricated!'

Melody smiled as he left the room, then got up to help herself to some juice. There were only two other people left eating their meal—certainly there was no sign of Adam. *Good*, she thought. Let's hope he makes himself scarce—at least while Jason is here. She frowned as she returned to her table. Jason was going to leave London as early as he could, and would ring her at some point to let her know when he expected to arrive. Melody bit her lip. She'd be feeling so different if Eve and Jon had been able to come, she thought. Having Jason here by himself was going to be a bit too 'cosy'—as Adam had dryly pointed out. Still, it was too late to change anything, so she'd have to make the best of it, she thought philosophically.

Presently Callum came in with her eggs, and she glanced up at him. 'I've a favour to ask, Callum,' she said.

'Name it,' the man said. 'It's yours!'

'Could I borrow something suitable to put fruit in?' she said. 'I've decided to go down to the cottage and pick some of my gooseberries—they're practically falling off the branches, they're so ripe.'

'Of course—we've some plastic boxes that we keep specially for the purpose,' Callum said. He paused. 'Adam was saying that he was going to help you with all that,' he went on. 'It's a very time-consuming job.'

'Oh, I'll be fine on my own,' Melody said quickly. 'I've no other plans for today anyway—my friend won't be here until this evening… Oh, by the way—one of the rooms I booked isn't needed now, Callum…'

'No—I know that. It's okay, Mel—Adam told me about it last night.'

Melody looked at him quickly. No doubt she—and her business—had been one of the topics of conversation, she thought, when the two men had been chatting. Perhaps the main one! She'd have loved to be a fly on the wall!

Callum hesitated, as if he wanted to say something important—then thought better of it and turned to go. 'By the way,' he said over his shoulder as an afterthought, 'this dry spell is coming to an end. Rain is forecast for tomorrow—so you'd better get that fruit in asap!'

'Maybe it's time for me to go back to London, then,' Melody answered. 'Everything has to come to an end some time.'

Presently, she popped into the kitchen to pick up the boxes she'd need. The breakfast girl had already left, and Callum was sitting at the table doing his accounts. Without looking up, he said casually, 'Adam's gone visiting friends this morning—but he'll be back later. Shall I tell him where you are…what you're doing?'

Melody shrugged. 'If you like,' she replied, equally casually. Well, what else could she say? She couldn't say, *No, don't tell him anything. I don't want him to get close.* That would give him more importance than he deserved—or more importance than she wanted to give him. So she left without another word, and made her way down the drive to the cottage.

Callum had been right. It was taking ages to strip the gooseberry bushes. The stems were spiky and uncomfortable, and the sun was baking on the back of Melody's head and neck as she stooped and reached for the fruit. But by late lunchtime she'd filled two large boxes and felt it was time for a short break and a drink—because this was thirsty work.

Going into the cottage, she cupped her hands under the cold water tap in the kitchen and gulped one or two mouthfuls—there was nothing suitable to drink from. Then she wandered into her sitting room and sat down on one of the boxes which Adam had so thoughtfully provided the other day. Somehow she wasn't feeling good this morning, she acknowledged. The euphoria she'd felt ever since she'd purchased the cottage seemed to be edging away from her. Ever practical, Melody tried to take stock of what was going on in her head. Was she getting cold feet, doubting her own wisdom in buying an expensive property in an out-of-the-way area? she asked herself. Or was there something else going on to ruffle her happiness? She clicked her tongue, annoyed with herself at feeling momentarily downbeat. What had changed to knock her off that dizzy perch of delight? Maybe, she thought, it was the same thing that she'd heard people say about childbirth…after the thrill of producing the offspring came the baby blues!

Sitting there with the afternoon sunlight lapping around her, Melody leaned her head against the wall for a second and closed her eyes. She knew that if Eve and Jon had been coming today she wouldn't be feeling like this. They would have been excited for her, enthusiastic at her unusual recklessness, and they would have cheered her up…because they were like that. But Jason was something else. As far as Melody could remember he'd never expressed the slightest interest in buying property—in fact, she didn't know much about him at all. She'd told Adam that he was a 'sort of' boyfriend, but that had been a deliberate lie. They'd never been close—he was just another member of her team—and that was why she'd been surprised when he'd insisted that he'd be coming down here alone today.

A sudden footstep by her side brought Melody back from having almost fallen asleep. She nearly fell off the box she was sitting on, and, looking up quickly, saw Adam standing there.

'Don't get up on my account,' he said smoothly. He pushed the other box to one side and sat down, facing her. 'Callum told me you were fruit-picking—d'you want some help?'

Melody stared at him for a moment, realisation hitting her like a crack on the head. Why had she been trying to find excuses for her present state of mind? she asked herself. Because the reason was sitting there beside her, gazing at her now with those bewitchingly dark eyes, his faintly cynical, murderously seductive expression melting any defence she could muster to protect herself from him. To protect herself from wanting him.

She hadn't answered him, so he repeated the question, but in a slightly different way. 'Shall we go and pick some more gooseberries?' he asked gently, tuning in to her vulnerability. 'I noticed that there are lots more on the bushes.'

'In a minute,' Melody said listlessly. 'I got rather hot out there—though Callum informs me that rain is on its way, so I suppose we'd better make the most of this sun while we've got it.'

'Have you had any lunch?' he asked suddenly, thinking how washed-out she looked, and that she might even be suffering from a mild touch of the sun.

'Not yet,' she replied. 'I…I didn't think about it…'

'Then that's the next thing we're going to do,' he said firmly, taking her hand and pulling her to her feet. 'We'll go to the Rose & Crown for a light snack—it'll be cool in there… Oh, and by the way, I've printed off the photographs to show you. I think you'll like them. They'll be a good set to take back and show all your friends and other interested parties.'

Feeling distinctly light-headed, Melody was glad to be taken charge of. And although she didn't feel like anything to eat, Adam insisted that she nibbled at a little bit of his ploughman's platter at the pub—which she did, washing it down with a whole bottle of still water. Then they went back to Poplars.

'I'll bring the prints up to show you in a minute,' Adam said, as Melody went up the stairs to her room.

Languidly, she washed her hands and face, wishing that Adam wasn't so obviously going to be part of her afternoon—but she realised that there was still all that fruit to pick, and it was kind of him to offer his help. Presently he knocked on her door, and came in with a folder under his arm.

'Have a look at these,' he said, darting a quick glance at her and thinking how white-faced she still was. He laid the prints out side by side in two rows on her bed, and Melody was surprised at how attractive they were. Even devoid of any of the usual trappings of glamorous lighting and expensive furniture, the cottage looked a desirable place to live in. The angles of the rooms Adam had chosen to take showed a pretty, slightly ancient dwelling, with huge potential as a comfortable place to live. Even the bathroom looked inviting enough!

'Adam—it all looks so good!' she exclaimed. 'And so much bigger!'

'Well, the sitting room is actually quite large for that type of place,' he said. 'And of course there's plenty of space outside for future extension—if you want it. Callum always envisaged a conservatory to open out on to the garden…if he'd ever owned it,' he added, not looking at her.

Melody swallowed, then stood back. 'Well, these are a fantastic representation of it for me to show everyone,' she said. She paused. 'I suppose we'd better get back to the gooseberry bushes…'

'You're going nowhere,' Adam said. 'You need to lie down, Mel, and have a sleep. Leave the bushes to me.'

She sat down weakly on the edge of the bed. 'D'you really mean it? D'you mind? It seems a bit off for me to relax while you sweat it out.' But the fact was she felt that if she never saw another gooseberry it would be too soon!

'Well, there you go,' he said cheerfully. 'I'll be your willing slave. But I'll expect my wages.'

Melody couldn't be bothered to think of a quick, slick reply to that—or even to wonder if there was any significance in his remark. Because her priority now was to lie down and chill out…

'Mel—your friend's arrived. He's waiting for you downstairs.'

Callum's voice outside her door woke Melody from the deepest sleep she could ever remember having, and with a start she jumped off the bed. 'Thanks, Callum. I'll be down in five minutes.'

She washed rapidly and slipped into a cream cotton sundress—then had to spend several minutes trying to brush the tangles from her hair. Pausing briefly, she recalled how Adam had done this exercise for her on the beach, and she shivered as she remembered the feel of his fingers threading their way gently but firmly through the thickness of the strands. Then, thrusting her feet into her loafers, she went quickly down the stairs.

Jason was standing by the front door, staring out, and he turned to see her.

'Hi, Mel! You look good enough to eat!' He automatically hugged her to him, and Melody lifted her cheek for the customary kiss of greeting which he obviously expected—feeling distinctly awkward as she did it. The man was nothing special to her, and she soon pulled away.

'Jason—you made it!' she said. 'But I didn't get a call from you to let me know when you'd be arriving…'

'I texted you—twice,' he said. 'Didn't you get my messages? To tell you I was being held up?'

Melody realised that she'd been so deeply asleep she'd not been aware of a thing!

Jason ran his hand through his hair. 'God—what a journey! I thought I was never going to get here.'

'Oh—was it that bad? Poor you…' Melody said soothingly, thinking how pathetic he sounded, almost petulant.

'There were two sets of roadworks on the motorway,' he went on complainingly, 'which meant all the traffic had to be diverted off—and when I eventually got away and into the countryside I felt as if I was taking part in an orienteering exercise!' He looked down at her. 'Did you deliberately try to find the most inaccessible holiday destination known to man?

Melody stared back at him, thinking how different he seemed. Casual wear didn't improve his appearance, she thought instinctively. He looked far better in a smart suit and tie. And where had his good humour gone?

She shrugged. 'Well, you're here now—' she began.

'Yes—and it's a good thing I was able to leave London earlier than I'd thought,' he said. 'Otherwise who knows what time it'd have been?'

Melody glanced at her watch. 'I take it you've checked in?' she said. 'Is your room okay?'

'Yes it's…okay,' he said, non-committally. 'But I haven't eaten since breakfast. I hope there's somewhere decent for supper?'

Melody sighed inwardly. This was going to be even worse than she'd thought. 'There is quite a nice pub,' she said. 'But wouldn't you like to see my cottage first, before we eat?'

He hesitated. 'All right—is it far from here?'

She smiled. 'Just a stroll. Takes about three minutes.'

Together they went down the drive, with Jason looking around him, taking it all in. 'This is an extremely isolated spot,' he said doubtfully.

'Yes—isn't it wonderful?' Melody countered. 'So blissfully peaceful.'

They arrived at the cottage, and Melody stood by the gate, spreading her arms. 'Behold!' she exclaimed. 'My holiday retreat…my rural castle!'

'Um…very nice,' Jason said unconvincingly. 'Smaller than I'd imagined, from what you said to Eve on the phone.'

'Well, there is only me,' Melody pointed out. 'And there's plenty of space for an extension—if I ever decide I need one.'

Inside, she took him around with as much enthusiasm as she could muster—because the vibes she was getting were distinctly unfavourable, and it was putting her off.

'Well, at least it's nice and clean,' he said, as they went from room to room.

'That's because it's been thoroughly scrubbed from end to end!' Melody exclaimed.

Upstairs, she pointed out at the garden. 'Just look at all those apples and pears!' she said. 'I'll be able to have my very own Harvest Festival! There's nothing like fruit really fresh, straight from the tree…'

'Yes, but what are you going to *do* with it all?' Jason said. 'There's masses of everything, and it'll take ages to pick—and who's going to eat it? Of course it would be fine for a family with a few kids, but there's far too much for one person.'

Melody looked at him, genuinely disliking him at that moment. It was all too clear that the man was no country-lover, and now that she thought about it, all his interests seemed to be city-based. She bit her lip. His reason for wanting to come down this weekend had to be more to do with seeing *her*, she thought with a sinking heart, and she cursed herself for having suggested he come along.

She could see at once that Adam had practically stripped the gooseberry bushes, but he'd obviously long gone.

After a few more minutes looking around—during which Jason seemed determined to point out every disadvantage he could think of—she said lightly, 'Well, perhaps it's time to go to the pub.'

'I'll second that,' Jason replied. 'I hope I'm going to be able to buy you something other than the ubiquitous pie and chips?'

He encircled her waist with his arm, and for a horrible moment Melody thought he was going to kiss her—properly. She pulled away neatly. He obviously didn't think much of her cottage, and she was beginning to think even less of him!

In the Rose & Crown she immediately saw Adam and Callum, sitting in the corner having a meal. Thinking it only polite, she went over and introduced Jason to Adam—he'd obviously already met Callum on his arrival—before making her way to another table a little way away.

'Who's the guy?' Jason asked, nodding briefly in Adam's direction.

'I told you. He's called Adam,' Melody said casually.

'Yes, but who is he? A local?'

'No. He's here on holiday. Like me.' She paused. 'He's been very kind—helping me with stuff, picking some of those gooseberries.'

'How very thoughtful of him,' Jason said cynically. The way Adam had looked at Melody just now had told its own story, and Jason deliberately made a fuss of pulling out Melody's chair for her, whispering something in her ear as he did it.

Melody tried very hard to enjoy the evening. She knew Adam was watching them out of the corner of his eye throughout the meal, sizing the situation up. Remembering why she'd asked Jason here in the first place, she had no option but to pretend she was having a good time. So now and then she leaned forward animatedly, feigning interest in all Jason was saying, and laughing occasionally at one of his 'jokes'—which were getting less funny with every glass of wine he was consuming. But she did manage to eat her prawn salad and half of a jacket potato—though Jason didn't seem to enjoy his food at all, complaining that the steak was overdone and tasteless.

By the time they got back to Poplars it was late, and she turned to look up at Jason. 'I hope you find your room comfortable, Jason, and that you have a good rest after your night-mare journey here—' she began lightly. But he caught hold of her, almost roughly.

'Oh, come on,' he said. 'Surely you don't expect me to sleep all alone in a big old strange house—not after having driven several hundred miles for the privilege.' He brushed the top of her head with his lips. 'You're looking so gorgeous, Melody,' he murmured. 'It would be such a waste for you to be unaccompanied tonight.'

Melody wrenched herself away from his grasp. 'I'm sorry, Jason, if you got the wrong idea about coming down—' she began, but he interrupted again.

'It was your suggestion,' he reminded her testily.

'Yes, because I thought you—and the others—would be interested in seeing what I'd been up to on my holiday…and in sharing in my excitement. But it's obvious that you are not. And *I* am certainly not interested in sharing my bed with you—or anyone else. Not tonight. Not ever!'

# CHAPTER TEN

MELODY was feeling the same unutterable loneliness that she'd felt in the days and weeks after losing first her mother and then Crispin. Once again she was by herself, not knowing which way to go or what to do.

Since she'd shut her door very firmly on Jason earlier, and heard him stomp crossly downstairs to his own room, she'd just stood by her window staring out across the orchard.

When she'd bought Gatehouse Cottage she'd felt without any doubt at all that she'd done the right thing—felt that an unseen hand had guided her to do it. But tonight she felt almost overwhelmed by negative thoughts.

She tried to reason with herself. She had invested in something which would never devalue—that was obvious. Property wasn't like expensive cars or holidays. Property lasted—and while people lived and breathed, the demand for it would never cease. So at least all that money she'd spent was intact. But investment had not been her first thought when she'd bought it. What had filled her heart and soul was the thought of being the owner of that very particular cottage, with all its associations, and the feeling that she belonged there, even though she had no memory of it. But now Jason—a man she knew so little of outside work—had made her confidence crumble, made her wonder whether her long sunny holiday had knocked her off balance. Had made her act impulsively and out of character by spending all that money.

And whether it was because she hadn't felt well all day, or because of the evening she'd spent with Jason during which he'd spelt out all his numerous reservations about what she'd done, Melody felt herself disintegrate inside. Without any warning her eyes misted over and filled with tears, and she sank down onto her bed and sobbed quietly, her shoulders shaking. As if in harmony with her mood, she heard the rain which had been forecast starting to patter against her windowpane.

A light tap on her door made her freeze for a second, and she leaned across to the bedside table and grabbed several tissues, rubbing fiercely at her eyes and nose.

'Yes?' she said. 'Who is it?' It had to be Jason, trying his luck a second time, she thought. Well, she would not open her door. But she went across and stood there for a moment. 'Who's there?' she asked tremulously.

'It's me—Adam.' His voice was low, and with a gasp of something that could only be described as relief Melody opened the door.

He came in quietly, closing it behind him. Then stood looking down at her for a few seconds. 'What's the matter, Mel?' he asked.

That did it. Melody started sobbing all over again.

After a minute or two, when he sensed that she was becoming calmer, he said, 'Now, are you going to tell me what this is all about?'

She went across to the bed and slumped down heavily. 'Oh, it's just…it's just Jason,' she said, her voice muffled into another tissue.

Adam stiffened—he'd thought as much! 'Why—what's he done? He hasn't tried anything on, has he? Something you didn't appreciate?' he said.

'No—no, it's nothing like that.' Melody sniffed.

Adam thought, 'Well, *I'm* surprised he's not here in your bed…you seemed to be having a pretty good time this evening!'

'Oh, I don't know, Adam,' Melody went on. 'He arrived here in a foul mood today, but the things he said about the cottage…about me choosing to have a place down here…'

'Well, what *did* he say?' Adam demanded.

'How long have you got?' Melody said, the trace of a watery smile on her lips. 'Firstly that it's in the back of beyond, and that even without undue traffic problems it's always going to take for ever to get here.'

'That's why we like it,' Adam retorted. 'To keep people like him away.'

'Also that I'd have to arrange for someone to look after the place for ninety per cent of the time because our work does tie us to London more or less permanently.' She reached for another tissue. 'And I must accept that there's some truth in that.'

'Go on,' Adam said.

'And he doesn't think much of the design of the place—thinks it's plain and uninspiring. Nothing to get so excited about.' She blew her nose and looked up. 'And he reckons I'll have to find someone—an agent, I suppose—to keep going in and out, especially in bad weather, to make sure everything's okay. Looking out for burst pipes, or squatters seizing the chance of taking up residence in unoccupied premises.'

Now that she'd started Melody couldn't stop, letting all the words pour out in a litany of misery.

'And he thinks there's far too much ground—too labour-intensive, according to him,' she went on. 'And that I'll have to employ a gardener more or less full time—certainly in the spring and summer—and that all the fruit trees are far too much for me to deal with, and that in any case I'll never be able to eat all the produce—which is obviously not meant for one person.'

'Anything else?' Adam asked dryly. 'Any more astute observations?'

'Just that he thinks there are far more suitable properties nearer town—more up-market, more "with-it", to use his expression. He thinks Gatehouse Cottage is in a sort of time-warp. In fact to him it's spooky. That's what he thinks.' She turned her face and looked up into Adam's eyes. 'I know I shouldn't take any notice of him, but I'm afraid all his remarks have left me feeling shattered.' She paused. '*You* think I was right to buy, don't you?' she pleaded.

Adam waited for a moment, longing to place his lips over her long wet eyelashes, thinking that in all the times they'd been together he'd never seen her look so lovely. So desirable. Then he pulled himself together sharply. She and Jason were obviously very close, judging by their tactile behaviour earlier, and Jason undoubtedly expected his opinion to be requested—and valued. Too bad if she didn't like what he said, Adam thought, trying not to remember the ridiculous tremor of jealousy he'd felt when he'd seen the man's hand cover Mel's. And then he suddenly thought of Fee, lying so hopefully in her hospital bed, and Callum, whose ambitions to own Gatehouse Cottage had been thwarted by this complete stranger.

He paused before answering Melody's question. 'Well, it's not for me to say, Mel,' he said coolly. 'That's something only you can decide in the end. But I suppose some of Jason's remarks do have the ring of truth.' He shot her a quick glance. 'There are always going to be problems with any venture, and you just have to accept that.' He paused. 'It's true that when we were chatting in the pub—you know, on the day of the auction—I did wonder whether you'd be able to make full use of your investment. Whether you'd ever be able to spend quality time down here…'

He didn't want to look at her as he spoke, feeling like an executioner. But after all, he consoled himself, it wasn't he who'd thrown cold water all over her tonight, it was her outspoken friend who'd done that. He turned away, his hands in his pockets. Could this after all turn things around for Fee and Callum? It meant so much more to them than it could possibly do for Mel… She'd obviously acted on the spur of the moment when she'd bid for the place—she'd soon find something else to take her fancy. The village didn't mean a thing to her. She didn't belong. Not like they all did.

He cleared his throat. 'I suppose your…bloke…*might* have appreciated being let in on your rather dramatic decision to cough up so much money—you know, before you actually did it?' he suggested. He paused. 'But—hey—don't get so upset, Mel,' he said cheerfully. 'If you do decide to change your mind, I'll take the cottage off your hands! After all, you only beat me at the auction by a whisker, didn't you? But you're a woman of firm convictions. I'm sure you'll make the right decision in the end.'

Slowly Melody got up, and went over to stand by his side. 'You're right—I will!' she said harshly. 'And thanks a bunch for the ringing endorsement! So you're clearly of the same opinion as Jason—but why should I be surprised? Men don't like being beaten at anything—not by a woman. I outbid you, and you didn't like it! Well, you and Jason can both go and take a flying leap! Gatehouse Cottage is mine, *mine*—whatever anyone else thinks! And I'll make it work—don't you worry about that! When I make up my mind about something— anything—I never change it!'

She stood away, glaring up at him. Gone was the pale face and watery eyes. Her cheeks were glowing with emotion.

'As far as my money is concerned, that's as safe as houses— ha-ha! And as for the "drawback" of this location—I'll deal with that! Yes, I may be dominated by my work calendar, but everyone can expect time off at regular intervals, and I shall treat my breaks in exactly the same way as I do my business commitments. Virtually unbreakable.' She paused for breath, but didn't give him a chance to interrupt. 'And have you ever noticed,' she went on, 'how any journey becomes less of a problem once it's familiar? I'll get to know every bend and twist in the road like the back of my own hand! And to know that my little house in the woods is here, waiting for me—well, the wheels won't turn fast enough!'

Adam stared down into her face, marvelling at her transformation over the last few minutes. This was one determined woman!

'As for finding someone to look after the cottage while I'm away… Well…I'll ask Callum to be janitor. And if he agrees I'll make it more than worth his while. If he's too busy, I'm sure someone in the village will oblige.' She tossed her head. 'Money talks,' she added. 'And the same goes for the garden and the trees. I'll be bringing friends down every summer to help with some of the fruit-picking—they'll think it's a real laugh, something away from the norm—and what we can't do ourselves I'll *pay* someone to do!' She held Adam's gaze defiantly. 'I can't think what came over me earlier,' she said. 'In my line of business we don't have problems—we only have opportunities! And that's what this is going to be! An opportunity for change—for me to have another life away from work and the pressures of living in London.' She turned on her heel. 'Now I need to get to bed. So goodnight, Adam!'

By now, it was gone midnight, and Adam went down the stairs to his own room on the ground floor. Going over to the window, he stared out across the garden—which was by now sparkling with the teeming rain—his mind going over the last hour. He'd only offered to go up to the second floor to save Callum doing it—who always made a point of checking outside all the rooms to make certain that all was well for the night before retiring himself—and then he'd heard Mel crying. He'd hated hearing it... Not that it had been any of his business, whatever it was.

Going into the bathroom, he undressed quickly and switched on the shower, glancing at his appearance in the mirror, which was rapidly starting to steam up. Looking objectively at his own face for a moment, he felt that he was trying to tell himself something... Shrugging, he stepped into the shower, letting the hot jets strike his tanned, athletic body harshly, making him tingle all over, making him feel alert and alive as he soaped himself vigorously. In his mind's eye he could still see Mel's tear-stained cheeks, and he wished that she was there now, as naked as he was. The anger and resentment which had flared up in her so unbelievably quickly had only added to her seductive charm, enflaming his own passion, making him want to press her soft curves to his hard, muscular body and lie with her in the soft folds of his bed. And make love to her.

His lip curled at the thought. That was about as unlikely to happen as the sea losing its salt!

With a huge white towel slung carelessly across his shoulders, he suddenly stopped what he was doing and stood quite still for a second. What was going on here? Had he *completely* lost the plot? After everything he'd vowed to himself—and confided to Callum—he'd never let another woman make a fool of him. But he knew he wanted to do more than just take Mel to his bed. He wanted to take care of her. Of course he'd wanted her from the first moment they'd met—that was merely par for the course in his life, the invariable rule when he met a beautiful woman. But that superficial, transitory sensation was turning into something far more dangerously fundamental and life-affirming. He *liked* her—big-time. And he still wanted her. How could it have happened with someone he'd known for such a short time? What about the expression 'once bitten, twice shy'?

Dropping the towel, he reached for his dressing gown,

padding barefooted into his bedroom. Naked, he threw himself down on the bed and stretched out his hands behind his head. He felt annoyed with everything—annoyed with himself. He'd lost the cottage, he'd lost his determination to resist the lure of the female sex, and now he'd lost the camaraderie which had existed between him and Mel. She'd seemed as furious with him as she was with Jason, seeing his remarks as a total lack of support. And, highly perceptive as she was, she would have easily recognised the whiff of opportunism when he'd said he'd take the cottage off her hands. He was left with nothing. Why hadn't he kept his big mouth shut?

Turning over, he thumped his pillow irritably. It was time to get away from here. His holiday was at an end.

Melody lay quite still in her bed, the duvet pulled up around her neck and shoulders like a cosy cocoon. Although she was still half asleep, a thousand thoughts and emotions wove themselves in and out of her head. Then suddenly her eyes flew open and alarm bells rang out in her head. She had spent the night in a dream world—and *what* a world! A world full of a heart-stabbing mix of tangled accusations and recriminations, where she had faced Adam like a prize fighter squaring up for the battle of her life!

They had each been holding the end of a thick rope and pulling, tugging, *tugging*… She'd actually felt her hands burning as she'd clung on desperately as it threatened to slip from her grasp. But he'd been far stronger than her, and little by little he had gained ground until, after what had seemed like hours of frustrated effort, she'd been pulled towards him fiercely—and she'd thought he was going to strangle her! To wind the length of vicious, knotted string around her neck. She'd gasped out loud. He had won! He was the victor! He had captured her, and his black eyes had stared down at her dangerously, his low, overpoweringly sexy voice whispering in her ear.

'The cottage will not be yours for much longer,' he'd hissed. 'You'll never live there. It's mine now, Mel, and so are *you*! There's no escape—we both know it—so why don't you just accept the inevitable and give in? Give in to me, and what *I* want!'

And suddenly the rope had vanished, and all she'd been able to feel was his arms around her, crushing every last breath from her body as their lips met in a frenzy of passion.

She sat up now, trembling all over. Trembling with the knowledge that she had not wanted to wake up, that she had wanted to go on and on dreaming... But she knew that this was all wrong, *wrong*! What had happened to her since she'd met Adam Carlisle to make her feel so emotionally captured and vulnerable? she asked herself. Because she was horribly aware that, in spite of all her determination to go solo for the rest of her life, she seemed to have slipped so easily within his inescapable radius.

Drawing her legs up, she rested her head on her knees. She was convinced that he had no significant interest in her—and why would he? With his looks and heart-throbbing sensuality he could flit from flower to flower as he liked—and fly off again. No problem! And anyway, during much of their time together they'd been engaged in housework, which had hardly set a peal of sexual bells ringing!

Yet during the passing of the night she had entered a forbidden world with Adam. They had lain together, and the first tentative touch of his hands on her bare skin had made her long for the unexplored, unimaginable excitement of what was to come. He was with her still, clearly... Her dream had not filtered away and been lost, but was still real, tangible.

His face, with the expansive brow, achingly seductive eyes and that faintly cynical half-smile which always filled her with a breathless intensity, had looked down at her as she'd lain beneath him. And when he'd told her that he would never let her go from his life, she'd known that she would have given herself to him freely. And when he'd declared that they were meant to be together always she had looked up at him, drinking in his every word, longing to believe that everything he was saying was true. And her lips had parted, moist and inviting, as he'd bent to cover them with his own, the hardness of his body against her sending a terrifying thrill of anticipation right through her, which even now refused to go away, leaving her with a desperate longing for it to have been true.

It was the memory of that all-defining moment of acute desire which now made Melody throw back her duvet and climb quickly out of bed. It wasn't too late, she thought, no real harm had been done. If she took action now, today, she could put a stop to this madness and get her life back on track.

It must have been raining all night, because as she drew back the curtains the dripping leaves and branches presented a rather dismal sight, totally different from the one she'd been so used to. Gone was the soft mellowness of warm, dry foliage. Everything looked sodden, cool and uninviting, and Melody heaved a sigh. What on earth were she and Jason going to do with themselves today? she thought. This was the first time on her holiday that the weather had presented a problem. She frowned, remembering the evening they'd spent together. They'd parted company very tight-lipped, but had agreed—rather frostily—to meet for breakfast at nine o'clock. She sincerely hoped that he was in a better mood today… Maybe he *had* been overtired, she thought, trying to find excuses for him, which would have been the reason why he'd been so negative about the cottage and everything else. Still, she thought, he had behaved very childishly, and had shown a side to him she'd found totally unpleasant.

She showered and dressed, feeling downbeat and faintly disoriented. Perhaps she'd suggest they'd go for a drive into the country, find a pub to have lunch. She stopped what she was doing for a moment, thinking of Adam, and how he'd added his own unwelcome comments when he'd found her crying. Well, she didn't want to see him today. Especially with Jason there. She knew he always breakfasted early, so hopefully they wouldn't bump into each other. She knew she'd find it horribly embarrassing for them all to come face to face.

But, taking everything into consideration, her mind was clear about one thing. She was leaving here as soon as possible. It was time to give up and move on. She would leave her beloved little cottage to its own devices, just for a few weeks—a cooling-off period she'd call it—and let her heart settle back into its normal passive state. Of course she couldn't go until Jason had left, but she'd pack most of her things now, in readiness. She needed to get back to London, where work was the only thing that absorbed her mind. Kept her sane and in control.

She emptied the wardrobe of her clothes, packing all her suitcases neatly, and cleared the chest of drawers. She could leave at a moment's notice, she thought.

Downstairs, Jason was already sitting at her usual table, and Melody could see that he was still rattled. He didn't bother to make a pretence of getting to his feet, or move her chair for her to sit down, but somehow Melody managed a weak smile of greeting.

'Hi,' she said, looking across at him quickly.

'Oh—hi,' he said casually.

'Did you sleep okay?'

'Not bad. Thunder woke me a couple of times.'

'Really? I didn't hear it,' Melody said, picking up her menu.

'Fantastic day,' Jason said sarcastically, glancing out of the window. 'What does anyone *do* in weather like this? Can we go to the gym for the morning, and then have a swim in the Olympic-size pool?'

Melody didn't bother to rise to that. 'I could show you a bit of the countryside—' she began, and he cut in.

'No, thanks. I saw quite enough of that yesterday.'

Just then Callum arrived to take their order, and Melody was so pleased to see his smiling face she could have hugged him. He grinned down, throwing her a mildly conspiratorial look that lifted Melody's spirits briefly.

After they'd finished their meal, Jason sat back, throwing his crumpled napkin down in front of him. 'Well, the breakfast wasn't bad,' he said grudgingly. 'And very generous.'

Melody looked across at him blankly. 'Do you know, Jason, that's the first positive remark you've made since you arrived here,' she said quietly.

He returned her look unblinkingly. 'What d'you expect?' he said. 'I didn't drive all that way to admire nature—or unremarkable boxes for living in—it was another side of creation that dominated my mind.'

He paused, and Melody thought, Why did I ever like you? Why did I ever think you were a nice guy, and fun to work with? She feigned innocence at his remark. 'Perhaps you'd explain?' she said.

'Come off it,' he snapped, still staring across at her. 'I know you've got a reputation for being a mysterious sort of woman, but I didn't think you were a tease.'

'A tease?' Melody frowned, mystified.

'Oh, I know all about women like you,' he went on coolly, as if they were discussing a cure for the common cold. 'Give out the signals, then do the disappearing trick. Offer the apple— whip it away. Naughty, naughty!'

Melody's jaw dropped in disbelief as he went on.

'You asked me here for the weekend, and I naturally thought we were going to have a good time together…'

She had had enough. 'What you "naturally thought" is your

problem!' she said heatedly, the blood rushing to her cheeks. 'I invited Eve and Jon down because I knew *they'd* be interested, and it occurred to me that maybe you might be, too!'

Melody crossed her fingers as she said that, knowing that she *had* had a certain agenda in including him—but not the one he was talking about!

She leaned forward so that her face was close to his. 'Watch my lips, Jason,' she said tersely. 'The idea that you and I might ever, *ever* share a bed was further from my mind than the idea of taking a walk to the North Pole in my nightie!' She sat back. 'And I consider it highly presumptuous of you to think so!' Thoroughly upset, she got up, pushing back her chair. 'I don't think it's a good idea for us to spend any more time together,' she said. 'And—'

'On that point we agree,' he replied, lounging back. 'I've already settled my bill—I'll be driving home this morning. It might not be too late to salvage something of the weekend.' He paused. 'And by the way—I forgot to tell you. I'll be handing in my notice at the office. I've decided that life's too short to work in a madhouse.'

Back in her room, Melody finished packing methodically, her hands still trembling slightly at the run-in she'd just had with Jason. What a loser, she thought angrily—and what a nerve, thinking he had a fling lined up for himself! Well, he knew the score now, and thank goodness they wouldn't have to see each other any more. In their line, when staff gave notice the parting of the ways usually happened overnight—to the advantage of everyone concerned. He'd been a very weak member of the team, in any case, she thought. He wouldn't be missed.

To her great relief there'd been no sign of Adam, and now, feeling upset and distracted, she went downstairs to find Callum. He was in the kitchen, and he looked up as she came in.

'Mel! Come and sit down.' He pulled out a chair, glancing at her quickly. 'Your…friend has checked out. I hope everything was okay for him…?'

''Oh, he found no fault with you and Poplars,' Melody said at once. 'The fault was all mine, Callum!' She paused. 'I'm glad he's gone,' she said firmly. 'The proverbial wet blanket, and a creep to boot.'

Callum looked away. 'Yes…I think that Adam was a bit concerned about you last night—you know, in the pub. He wondered…'

Melody shook her head briefly. 'It's okay, Callum—I can take care of myself. But it was kind of Adam to be bothered on my account.'

Callum looked at her steadily. 'I think he's a bit more than just bothered about you, Mel,' he began, and she cut in—she didn't want to hear any more.

'I'm really sorry—but I'm leaving later as well, Callum,' she said slowly. She took the cottage keys from her pocket. 'Would you do me a tremendous favour?' she asked. 'Would you keep these, and just look in at the cottage now and then? I'm not exactly sure when I'll be coming back—probably not until next month.'

'No problem.' Callum grinned. 'We've taken care of the place for so long now—all the time it's been empty—it'll make no difference. Leave it to us.' He looked down at her soberly. 'D'you really have to go?'

'Afraid so—there's a panic on at work, and I'm needed,' she lied.

'We'll miss you, Mel—really,' he said. 'Can't you wait until Adam gets back? He's having lunch with the de Wintons over at the big house—the Manor—across the valley, but he'll be home later, and I know he'd want to see you before you go.'

Melody stood up. 'No—I'm sorry to have to depart, but…it

can't be helped.' She hesitated. 'I'll leave Adam a note, explaining.' She slipped her bag from her shoulder. 'Now, let me settle my bill—and I've *loved* staying here, Callum. It's been like a home from home.'

'And we've loved having you,' Callum said. He waited before going on. 'I'm fetching Fee back from hospital on Monday—it's a shame she won't see you to say goodbye.'

Melody felt as if she was being pulled painfully in two directions—desperately wanting to stay, but knowing that she mustn't. Spending any more time with Adam was not the way forward. Not the way it had to be. 'I'm sorry,' she said quietly. 'Now—would you help me with my cases?'

Presently, driving back to London in the pouring rain, Melody found her mind going over and over everything that had happened during her holiday, and why she'd decided, at this particular time of her life, to go there at all. Of course it had been a personal mission, hoping to find answers to a mysterious part of her mother's life, but she'd learned nothing—nothing of significance had happened at all. Except the purchase of a cottage! *The* cottage! But she still didn't know why Frances had been so secretive about the man who was Melody's father.

It had been an idyllic few weeks, marred only by Jason's arrival on the scene—self-inflicted though that had been, she had to admit—but she still felt unsure of the wisdom of setting up a home for herself so far away from everything. It had seemed so right during her post-purchase honeymoon, but now all Jason's comments seemed to make some sense.

She pulled in to the side of the road for a moment, and reached for her bottle of water, drinking freely. Well, she had plenty of sustenance readily available if she needed it, she thought, smiling briefly and glancing down to the floor of the car at all the bags containing the gooseberries they'd picked.

She'd share those out as soon as she got back to work. She leaned her head back, taking another drink, and looking with unseeing eyes through the drenched windscreen. She'd have to arrange for all those apples, pears and plums to be gathered at some point. Not just this year, but every year from now on. In her position, the garden *was* a drawback—delightful though it had first seemed. And she'd confirm the date for the decorators to begin as soon as possible, and arrange for someone to sort out the windows… Blinds, or curtains, or both? she wondered.

She sighed, knowing that all this would have to be fitted in with her other life. And how much of that other life would release her to come down to her cottage? To relax, to chill out, to do all those things that were supposed to be good for you?

She put the cap back onto the bottle, squeezing it tightly. In spite of all these practical issues, she knew only too well what her real problem was. She couldn't risk letting Adam Carlisle penetrate her life, her sensibilities, any more than he had already done. He was the problem, not the cottage, because she admitted to herself that he had become more to her than she'd have thought possible, and she didn't want it. She didn't want him or any man. And, so far she'd succeeded perfectly well in that aim, ever since Crispin had been killed.

She switched on the engine decisively. She had been right to escape this morning, before seeing him. And although she realised that he would always be a visitor to the area, and that they would be bound to come across each other from time to time, it would never be the same as this had been. The novelty of everything that had happened over the last week or so would have worn off, died. And with it—hopefully—the unsettling thought that she was not as emotionally unassailable as she'd thought.

# CHAPTER ELEVEN

DESPITE the fact that she'd still had another week due to her, Melody returned to work on the following Monday. Anyway, it was quite nice to think she had some time in hand she could use up later in the year.

Eve and Jon were at their desks, desperate to hear about her holiday—and the cottage! Melody looked across at them both as she booted up her computer.

'The holiday was fantastic,' she said. 'The weather was perfect—right up until the very last day—and look: I've got some photographs of the cottage to show you.' She fished out from her briefcase all the prints Adam had prepared for her, passing them across. The others examined them closely—and were wildly enthusiastic, as Melody had known they would be.

'Mel—it's gorgeous! So quaint!' Eve said. 'Oh, look—*look*, Jon—look at the garden! It's a little paradise!'

'Yes, and the little paradise is full of gooseberries—among other things,' Melody said. 'I've got a load of them for you in my fridge. Enough for about fifty pies!'

Eve spread all the prints out on the desk in front of them. 'It looks just like the sort of place a small child would draw. Absolutely charming,' she said slowly.

'It's not all that big—' Melody began, and Eve interrupted.

'Who wants a mansion as a holiday retreat, for goodness' sake? Just so long as there's room for *us*—when we keep invading you!' She turned to Jon. 'Maybe *we* could look around for something down there?' she said eagerly.

'Maybe,' he agreed non-committally. *They* didn't have the financial resources that Mel seemed to have, he thought.

'I was desperately disappointed that you couldn't come down at the weekend,' Melody said, thinking how pale her friends were looking—or perhaps that was in contrast to *her* deep suntan!

'So were we,' Jon said at once. 'But we were not a pretty sight, Mel. We really succumbed to the wretched sickness bug that's swept the office. You were better off out of it, I can tell you.'

'Umm—pity Jason hadn't caught it as well,' Melody said enigmatically, and they both looked at her quickly.

'Yes—we were wondering about that,' Eve said. 'He insisted on going on with the plan.' She paused. 'You've heard that he's gone, by the way, rather suddenly?' she asked. 'Though he never really fitted in, did he? It wasn't a surprise when he made the big announcement.'

Melody made a face. 'He thought—wrongly—that he and I were going to enjoy a passionate weekend together,' she said, putting all the prints away carefully. 'And it gave me great pleasure to disabuse him on the point.'

The others burst out laughing. 'You're joking! What—you and *him*?' Jon exclaimed. 'Why on earth did he imagine that he would succeed where all others have failed? He must have been kidding himself if he thought he'd found the Holy Grail!'

Melody looked away. She remembered Jason's remark about her being 'mysterious', and she supposed that her unwillingness to engage in any romantic attachments would attract some criticism from the people she mixed with. Well, so be it, she thought. Her life was her own, to live as she liked, whatever anybody else thought.

Work had built up in her absence, as she'd known it would, and there wasn't time for much gossiping about her holiday. But that pleased Melody. She wanted to forget it all—temporarily at least—and use her brain for the thing it had been trained for. So it was late before she'd finished what she had to do, and everyone else had packed up and gone home by the time she left the building.

By now, she'd realised how tiring the day had proved, and decided to hail a cab rather than bother with the tube and the considerable walk to her flat.

Presently, after paying the driver, she was just inserting the key into her door when a low voice behind her made her jump anxiously. She turned quickly.

'Hello, Mel. I was beginning to think you weren't coming home tonight.'

'Adam!' Melody was genuinely amazed to see him standing there. 'What are you doing here? And how did you know—? I mean…'

'How did I know where you live? From all the details you gave to Callum when you checked in to Poplars, of course,' he said. He came to stand right beside her, and looked down into her upturned face. 'I have to go back to Malaysia tomorrow. But I had a meeting in London this afternoon and couldn't turn down the opportunity to look you up.' He paused. 'I hope I'm…I hope I'm not taking liberties,' he added slowly.

Melody thought desperately, Please don't touch me, Adam… Keep your distance, please! She shrugged. 'Of course not. Come in.' Her voice shook slightly. Well, she was tired— and she needed a drink and something to eat.

He followed her up the thickly carpeted stairs to her first-floor flat, which was spacious and luxurious, and looked around appreciatively as Melody switched on all the lamps. She threw her bag and briefcase down on to one of the huge sofas, and looked up at him.

'Drink?' she asked casually. 'There's some whisky.' Crispin's whisky, she thought. Still there, untouched.

'Whisky would be great, thanks,' he said. He'd barely taken his eyes off her, admiring her as he'd done so many times before. She looked trim and businesslike in her fine-quality black suit and ivory silk shirt, her black high heels making her look slightly taller than usual.

She paused. 'Everything's over there on the table,' she said. 'Help yourself. I must change into something I can relax in.' She turned away. 'It's been a long day.'

'I hope you were able to get the "panic" sorted out,' he said archly. 'You know—the thing that made you shoot off in such a hurry?' And Melody found herself blushing as she remembered what she'd written in the note she'd left him.

'Yes—I did get the…problem sorted, thank you,' she said flatly.

There was a distinct coolness in the atmosphere, and they both felt it. Well, after all, the last words they'd exchanged had hardly been the most friendly! But she did pause for a moment to look back at him, her face expressionless.

'I'm sorry I had to dash off like that—' she began.

'Not as sorry as I was,' he said, going over to pour himself some whisky, and Melody stared after him, wondering what was coming next.

He looked so stunning, she thought, swallowing, with his height, powerful frame and broad shoulders throwing huge shadows across the walls of the room. It was the first time she'd seen him formally dressed, she realised, and it added even more to his dynamic sex appeal. But what was he doing here, in the sanctity of her flat? she asked herself. She'd left Poplars early to get away from him. She'd never expected him to turn up here, uninvited.

He turned to look at her, his glass in his hand. 'I thought you were out of order to leave so abruptly,' he said coolly. 'Surely whatever it was that was so urgent could have waited another couple of hours?' He drank from his glass. 'Or perhaps it was something else? Callum indicated that you and Jason had not been exactly—'

'It was nothing to do with Jason,' Melody interrupted coldly. 'I told you, I had to come back earlier than expected.'

'Well, I still think it was a rather off-hand way for you—for anyone—to behave,' he said shortly.

Suddenly Melody felt trapped—and annoyed. And she didn't like being spoken to like a child, either. 'I'm sorry if it didn't please you,' she said shortly, 'or if you took it the wrong way. But what's done is done.' She turned abruptly. 'I shan't be long. Make yourself at home.'

In her bedroom, feeling completely dazed—not to say shattered—at Adam turning up, Melody slipped out of her office clothes and shrugged into her navy tracksuit. Then she undid her hair from its knot, running her brush through it briefly and leaving it loose around her shoulders. She didn't bother to find her mules, but walked barefoot across the thick pile of her carpet to open the door, pausing for a moment. How was she going to get rid of him? she wondered—and then felt guilty. He hadn't behaved badly towards her, after all—not really, if you didn't count his unhelpful remarks about her purchase of the cottage, and his seeming to side with Jason. And if you didn't count him telling her off just now for her quick get-away from Poplars. Could she ever forget how he'd helped her scrub the cottage from end to end? There'd been no need for him to do that. Still, she hadn't got over the shock of finding him on her doorstep when she'd come home... He *could* have rung to warn her of his impending visit, she thought. That would have shown some consideration.

Biting her lip, she went across the dimly lit hallway and into the sitting room, where Adam was studying Crispin's huge globe of the world on its imposing mahogany stand. He glanced up as she came over to join him, and he caught his breath. Why did everything the woman wore glamourise her? he asked himself. There was nothing exceptional about the thing she had on—except that it had the effect of making him want to gather her up in his arms and mould her to him.

'What a beautiful object,' he said, turning back to the globe, revolving it slowly.

'Yes. It was my present to Crispin on his last birthday,' she said soberly.

He gave her a quick glance, feeling the need to lighten the mood. 'Would you like to see where I spend most of my working life?'

She looked down as he traced his finger over the smooth surface.

'See…there it is. Malaysia. A very long way away…' He recognised the faint drift of her perfume as she peered down to see where he was pointing.

'I've never been that far away from home,' she said. 'In fact, I've not travelled very much at all—except skiing in France and Switzerland with our friends. When I was young, my mother and I liked holidays nearer home—when we could afford to go at all,' she added simply.

So it was obviously her husband's money that had bought all this, Adam thought briefly. Though their combined salaries must have been considerable.

'Oh, you'd like Malaysia,' he said easily 'The people are lovely. Who knows? I may have the chance to extend your knowledge of the world some day, and take you there.'

Melody looked up at him. That'll never happen, she thought.

'But before that,' he said smoothly, 'I'd like to take you somewhere for a meal.' He hesitated. 'You were so late getting home, I was afraid I was going to be dining alone this evening.'

Melody shook her head. 'Sorry—no. It's already gone nine, and I only eat very light meals in the week.' She hesitated. 'But I'd be happy to make us some omelettes. Cheese—or I think there are some prawns, if you prefer.' Her eyes twinkled for a second. 'I could even knock you up a full English. I come highly recommended!' she added.

'I'm fully aware of that,' he replied, and their eyes locked together, and somehow, suddenly, they were back to where they had been on those few hectic mornings in the kitchen at Poplars. They had shared a curious experience, and they'd both enjoyed it. And were enjoying the memory of it. 'I'll pass on the full English—though a cheese omelette sounds fantastic. Thanks.'

Melody went over and switched on the huge flat-screen television. 'Take your pick,' she said, handing Adam the remote control and going out in the direction of the kitchen.

'Can't I help?' he called after her.

'No, not this time,' she replied.

Going through the hall, she glanced into her dining room— it was not quite as large as the sitting room, but was an ample size to entertain ten or twelve guests at one go. But the room would not be used tonight. They'd eat from trays on their laps, she decided.

Melody knew exactly how to prepare a good omelette. It had always been one of her masterpieces! She cooked in butter, using two frying pans, and the eggs were soon ready for her to carefully lift them over and on to warm plates. She'd already cut thin slices of wholemeal bread to accompany them. Then she opened a bottle of white wine and selected two glasses from the shelf, before taking everything in.

Immediately Adam stood up and switched off the television, pulling a small table nearer to them for the trays, and presently, sitting side by side on the sofa, they made short work of their supper.

Adam was impressed as he swallowed the last morsel. 'Mmm, delicious,' he said. 'Funny that none of the guests ever asked for omelettes.'

Melody put down her own knife and fork, and sat forward to remove the two trays, but he put a hand briefly on her arm.

'Let me at least do the clearing away,' he said, getting up. He looked down at her. 'And am I allowed to make coffee? You know I do it so well!'

Melody smiled. 'Oh, go on, then,' she said. 'You'll find everything you need by the kettle.'

She watched as he made his own way to the kitchen—well, the geography of the place was hardly complex—suddenly realising how good it felt for someone else to be there, sharing in the task of even a simple thing like preparing the after-supper drinks, and remembering, with a pang, that that had always been Crispin's job. She heard Adam fill the kettle, take mugs from the shelf, open the fridge door for milk, and wondered again, how this could be happening. How had the man managed to thread himself into *this* part of her life as well?

In a few minutes he returned, with the cafetière and everything else on a tray, which he put down in front of them. 'This is a fabulous apartment, Mel,' he said casually. 'And so beautifully furnished.' He paused. 'I can easily see why Jason took such a dim view of the cottage. I'm sure he'd rather be staying here than there.'

'Well, it won't matter what he thinks,' Melody said, leaning her head back against the cushions. 'Because I won't be inviting him anywhere, ever again.'

Adam raised one quizzical eyebrow. 'Oh,' was all he said. But of course Callum had tipped him off about Mel's describing the man as a 'creep'. Clearly he'd put more than one foot wrong, Adam thought wryly.

'Finish the wine, Adam,' Melody said lazily. 'It'd be a shame to waste that last drop.'

He lifted the bottle, judging the contents. 'Oh, I think there's enough for us both to have half a glass,' he said.

Melody was slightly shocked to realise just how much she'd drunk—quite a lot more than her usual quota! But she allowed him to top up her glass before he emptied the rest into his own.

'Do these places come on the market very often?' he asked, without looking at her, and Melody thought, I hope you're not thinking of buying one yourself!

'Oh, now and then,' she said casually. 'They are at the top end of the market for this kind of place, but it seems there's no shortage of money, because as soon as one becomes vacant it's snapped up.' She looked across at him, her eyelids threatening to droop from the effect of the alcohol—and her fatigue after the long day. And, unusually for her, she felt her natural reserve slip. 'I never expected to be able to afford something like this,' she confided honestly. 'When I think of the little house I spent my childhood in…'

'I'm sure your husband left you well provided for,' he suggested gently.

'Yes,' she replied, feeling sad all over again. 'He was well insured.'

But surely, Adam thought, that would not explain how she'd been able to buy Gatehouse Cottage—she'd hinted at one point during a conversation that she hadn't had to borrow for it.

And as if reading his mind, she said, 'The cottage… I bought the cottage with a legacy left to me by the cousin of my mother's we used to live with. I had no idea she had any money—not that kind of money, anyway. We were always quite poor.' There—now she'd told him, Melody thought. So what?

Sitting close—but not too close to her on that enormous

sofa—Adam wished that he hadn't decided to come here tonight. She had reawakened that irrepressible desire in him that he knew would never be satisfied. Would never be fulfilled. Why hadn't he just left things as they were, gone back to the Far East tomorrow and tried to forget her? Time not only healed, sometimes it dealt with a problem, he thought. Let water run under the bridge. That way things often evened themselves out. But it was too late. He *was* here.

He tore his gaze away from her. 'I'm sure you want to know about Fee....' he began, and Melody sat forward with a jolt.

'Oh, of *course*!' she exclaimed. 'Dear Fee! How is she? Is she home?'

'Yes. I waited until Callum brought her back—waited to see how things were. They have high hopes this time.' He paused. 'I only hope they're right.'

Melody felt really bad for a second. She'd hardly given Fee a thought over the last two days, but it wasn't because she didn't care—she *did* care! It was just that she had so much stuff going on in her own life...

Adam leaned forward to pick up the cafetière and filled the two mugs, passing her one. 'I seem to remember you like cream?' he murmured, picking up the small jug he'd put on the tray. Without answering, she held her mug forward. For a while, there was silence between them as they sipped the delicious brew. Then Melody said, 'When do you go tomorrow?'

'I fly from Heathrow at eleven p.m.,' he said. 'For a twelve-hour haul to Kuala Lumpur.'

Melody frowned. 'That sounds an ordeal.'

'Not really,' Adam said. 'I use a superb airline. And the cabin staff—who always look beautiful in Malaysian national dress—are among the best in the world.'

Melody closed her eyes, feeling sleepy and relaxed. 'I suppose it's a very hot climate?' she said.

'Yes, it always is,' he replied. 'But there are things to compensate. You can go to Penang from Kuala Lumpur, to the Cameron Highlands, where it's much cooler—and where, incidentally, you can get delicious strawberry teas.' He turned to look at her again, noting that somehow they'd moved slightly closer together, so that he could smell the warmth of her skin, smell that particular fragrance in her hair which he'd recognise blindfold anywhere. 'It's an idyllic setting,' he went on softly. 'You'd love it. And there's an amazing butterfly population…' There was a long, uncomplicated silence before he whispered, 'Are you asleep, Mel?'

'No, of course not. I'm listening to you.' Listening to that voice which makes me want to curl up inside, she thought. She opened one eye and looked at him. 'Are the hotels any good?'

'The hotels are superb. I'd take you to a sumptuous hotel where you'd be treated like a princess… The food's amazing—mostly home-grown produce—and the national dish is satay—chicken or beef kebabs marinated in lime juice… The fruit, of course, is exotic—pineapples, papaya, bananas…'

Melody smiled faintly. 'You sound like an employee of the Malaysian Tourist Board,' she said.

He shrugged. 'It really is a great place,' he replied.

They both sat there, almost wallowing in the comfortable atmosphere which enveloped them. Then he said, 'So…have you any idea when you'll be going back to your "little house in the woods"?' he asked.

'Oh—not exactly,' she replied. 'But it'll be in the reasonably near future. There's all that fruit to be taken care of, isn't there?' She paused, needing to ask him roughly the same question. 'And you…when do you expect to be visiting Poplars again?' she said.

He shrugged. 'Not too sure at the moment. There's…there's a lot going on with the firm. So I really can't say.'

Presently, Melody said, 'Where are you staying tonight?'

Adam hesitated. 'I'm booked in at my father's club,' he said. 'That's where I've left my cases. I suppose I ought to be going...d'you have a taxi number handy?'

There was a moment's pregnant silence. Then, 'Stay here,' Melody said quietly, without looking at him. 'You do realise what the time is, don't you?'

'I know it's late,' he replied cautiously. He looked at her, an expression of disbelief crossing his features. He was being invited—*she* had invited him—to spend the night with her! His mouth dried at the prospect.

'Well, then—stay,' she repeated, her eyes still closed.

He put his hand gently over hers, and it excited him to feel her turn her palm and curl her fingers in response. Until a few moments ago he might have expected her to push him away! 'Are you...sure, Mel?' he asked softly. 'I mean—I could easily get a cab.'

'Oh, don't bother to do that,' she replied. 'It seems pointless at this time of night.' She gazed down at his strong brown hand where it covered hers. She and Crispin had always held hands as they'd watched television. Now she looked up at him, her lips slightly parted, her eyelashes bewitchingly moist. 'But you do understand that I'll be disturbing you in the morning? I'll have to leave before you've even surfaced...' she murmured.

Don't count on it, he thought to himself. He didn't think they'd be spending much of the night asleep in any case!

With a dainty yawn Melody got up, stretching her arms above her head languidly, and together they took the coffee things back into the kitchen, before switching off the lights and going across to the hallway. Melody put her hand on his arm briefly.

'You'll find the spare room very comfortable,' she murmured. 'Just look around you for anything you need.' She paused. 'I moved all Crispin's belongings into that room, because I haven't decided yet what to do with them. Feel free to help yourself—and there are plenty of toiletries in the bathroom.'

She reached up and planted the lightest of kisses on his cheek. Her lips were cool.

'Goodnight, Adam—sleep well,' she whispered. And with that she opened her bedroom door and went inside, closing it firmly behind her.

# CHAPTER TWELVE

'MEL? *Hello*, Mel! It's Fee here!'

Melody's face creased into smiles as she heard the woman's voice. 'Fee—how great to hear from you!' she said.

It was a Saturday morning in mid-September, and Melody, still in her dressing gown, was idly reading the daily paper as she sipped her first coffee for the day. 'How are you, Fee? Not overdoing things at Poplars, I hope?'

Fee chucked. 'Oh, I'm being treated like a queen, Mel. I'm following doctor's orders to the letter, and am glad to say that I've not had any recurrence of the symptoms I've had in the past.'

'That's fantastic!'

'Of course Callum would wrap me in cotton wool if he could,' Fee went on, 'but I know exactly how much I can do, and it's obviously good to keep active—within limits.'

'You must both be feeling very excited,' Melody said.

'Cautiously excited is how I'd describe it,' Fee replied. 'But listen, Mel…I never had a chance to thank you so, *so* much for what you did for us here, when I had to make that hasty trip to hospital,' she went on. 'We've never been caught out like that before, and Callum and I agree that if you and Adam hadn't stepped in to help us we'd just have had to apologise profusely to the guests and send them all on their way. An unthinkable prospect!'

Melody smiled. 'You know, Fee, we really enjoyed ourselves,' she said. 'Preparing breakfast for a crowd is never likely to faze me in the future!'

'Well, we'll always be grateful to you,' Fee said. She paused. 'You know, Adam described you as an unusual woman when he met you on that first day—and he was right. I can't think of many guests who'd be ready to put on an apron and get stuck in in an emergency!'

They chatted on for a few minutes, and Melody thought how good it was to hear Fee's warm and friendly voice again. It filled her with a rush of pleasurable homesickness. Why wasn't she there in the village now?

As if reading her thoughts, Fee said, 'But I've also rung to know about you, Mel, and when you're coming back to visit. We didn't even have a chance to say cheerio in the summer, did we?'

Melody made a wry face to herself. 'No—I'm sorry about that…sorry I had to dash off, Fee,' she said. 'But I *had* had a very long break, and all good things must come to an end—though the end was a bit sudden.'

'Well, of course we realise your work is important…we quite understood.'

That made Melody feel worse than ever!

'Now then,' Fee went on, 'is it possible you could come down for the last weekend of this month? That's when we have the Harvest Fair.'

'Oh—I remember you talking about that,' Melody said, getting up and wandering over to the window.

'It's one of *the* occasions in the village,' Fee said enthusiastically. 'It's always fun—and of course makes good profits for our various local charities. But more than that, Mel, it brings the community together in a wonderful spirit of goodwill... which has to be a good thing.'

'Of course,' Mel agreed, feeling slightly guilty at Fee's words. What had she, Melody Forester, done for the village so far? Precisely nothing, she thought. But that was going to change—she would be returning there as often as possible.

'There is something else,' Fee said. 'All the fruit in your garden is ready—especially the plums, which are absolutely gorgeous this year, thanks to our summer. Would you allow us to pick some of it to sell at the Fair?'

'Of course I would!' Melody said. 'It's been on my mind, as a matter of fact.'

'A few of the Boy Scouts from the local troupe would be happy to do it,' Fee said. 'If you like, they could pick everything for you, and we'd just keep a few basketfuls for the Fair. Would that be okay?'

'Sounds perfect,' Melody said, and without another thought, added, 'And I *will* come down on that weekend, Fee. I'll look forward to it.' She hesitated. 'Will you reserve me a room at Poplars, please—for three nights?'

Later, as she went around the flat tidying up, Melody realised that Fee had only mentioned Adam once... Well, he was probably sitting under a tree with a dusky Malaysian maiden, his mind a long way away from England, she thought.

She stopped what she was doing for a second. It seemed such a long time ago that he'd turned up here, totally unexpectedly. When she'd emerged from her bedroom the following morning he'd already been up and dressed. And the looks they'd exchanged had spoken volumes, with Adam's slightly raised eyebrow and quizzical expression making Melody's heart quicken—as usual. Yet there had been not a hint of awkwardness between them as they'd consumed coffee and toast in the kitchen, and he'd thanked her politely for a very comfortable night's sleep as they'd parted company in the street.

Two weeks later Melody found herself once more making the long drive south. She'd left work early, hoping to be at Poplars in time to take Fee and Callum out to supper. She had actually asked Eve and Jon to come with her, thinking that they'd enjoy the whole event, and the chance to see the cottage, but they were committed to attending a family wedding—much to Eve's dismay.

'When are we *ever* going to see it?' she'd grumbled.

'Don't worry,' Melody had said, 'there'll be plenty of other occasions. And I promise to bring you back loads of fruit!'

Now, with her favourite CDs playing, the late-afternoon sun shining—and good weather forecast for the weekend—Melody felt her spirits soar as she sped along the motorway. Although there *were* one or two traffic hold-ups—as Jason had so cynically predicted there always would be—it was just seven-thirty as she once again drove up the long drive of Poplars…to see Adam's red Porsche already parked! As soon as she saw it colour flooded Melody's cheeks. She'd not given a thought to the possibility that he might be here this weekend as well!

She pulled in alongside, and even before she could collect her things together Adam's strong footsteps crunched across the gravel towards her. He opened her door, smiling down at her darkly.

'Hello, Mel,' he said casually, as if she shouldn't be at all surprised at seeing him.

Was there a conspiracy going on here? Melody asked herself. But anyway, did it matter? They both had equal interests in the area, and it was a free world. She returned his smile.

'Well, hello, Adam,' she said. 'I didn't realise that…'

'Oh, didn't Fee tell you I was coming for a few days?' he asked lightly. He paused. 'I hope it isn't a nasty surprise, Mel?'

'Of course not. Don't be silly,' she replied quickly—with a

hint of *why should it matter to me whether you're here or not* in her voice.

He took her case from the boot, and together they went across to the entrance. Fee came out almost at once, automatically giving Melody a hug.

'Fee—you're looking absolutely blooming!' Melody said.

'Thank you,' Fee said. 'And if you actually mean that I'm looking plump—then say so! The pounds seem to be piling on!'

Together they went into the kitchen, where Callum was giving the dogs their supper. He immediately came over to Melody, his hand outstretched in greeting. Presently, the four sat around chatting, the dogs nudging Melody's legs for some attention.

'The fruit's all been taken care of,' Callum said. 'There was plenty for the Fair and more than enough for you, Mel!'

'Thanks for that,' she said gratefully. 'That's one thing sorted, at least.' She shot a quick glance at Adam. 'I didn't know that Adam would be here, too,' she said.

'Oh, didn't I mention that on the phone?' Fee said innocently. 'Adam usually tries to come back for this particular occasion—and this weekend is a very special one this year, in any case. More special than usual,' she added.

Melody raised her eyebrows. 'How so?'

'My parents are celebrating their Golden Wedding Anniversary,' Adam said. 'And they decided that here, among old sights and old friends, was where they wanted to spend it. At Poplars—their old home.'

'We've all known each other for such a long time,' Fee said. 'It's going to be like a big family get-together.'

Melody felt a sudden tightening in her chest. It seemed that she was probably going to meet people who would have known her mother, and the thought made her slightly panicky... But wasn't this what she wanted? she asked herself. Perhaps something, some little hint, might at last explain why Frances had never wanted to return here. And *she* could still keep the secret…because Melody's connection with the place was still not known by anyone. And it would stay like that for ever, if she wanted it to. No one need ever know that she was Frances's illegitimate daughter.

She smiled quickly. 'After I've unpacked my few belongings,' she said, 'I hope you'll allow me to take you to the Rose & Crown for supper.'

'Sorry, Mel, no can do,' Callum said, getting up. 'There are a few last-minute things I've got to sort out up at the village hall for tomorrow.' He paused. 'And I'm hoping that my wife will agree to have an early night. We've all been rather busy lately. But thanks for the offer.'

'I understand,' Melody said at once. 'And, judging by the cars, you're still pretty full.'

'Eight guests are due to check out in the morning,' Callum said. 'Then it'll be just Adam and his parents and you staying, Mel. And we can all relax.'

Adam stood and glanced down at Melody. 'I've picked up your key—allow me to show you to your room, madam.' He took her case from her. 'At least *I* can join you for supper— I'm not having an early night,' he added. 'My parents are visiting friends this evening,' he explained, as they went up the stairs. 'But they'll be very interested to meet the new owner of Gatehouse Cottage.'

Melody couldn't help feeling slightly bewildered. She'd come here in good faith, to take part in an annual ritual in the life of this village, but somehow Adam had stepped in from nowhere and was filtering himself into her life—again.

He opened her door and put her case down inside. 'I'm hungry,' he announced. 'See you downstairs in half an hour.'

In less than that time Melody ran quickly back downstairs. She'd not bothered to change out of the black jeans and pale grey shirt she'd travelled in, but had undone her hair, leaving it loose. Adam was waiting by the door, and looked up as she joined him. As always, her appearance, her femininity, stirred him, and without thinking what he was doing he took her hand lightly in his.

Melody looked up at him. 'Now,' she said firmly, 'this time supper really is on me. I shall insist.'

'Okay,' he replied easily. 'But at least let me drive us.'

As they made their way down the drive, Melody suddenly turned to him. 'Do—do you mind if we don't go to the Rose & Crown?' she asked tentatively, thinking of the evening she'd had to endure there with Jason. 'I'd rather go somewhere different.'

He glanced back at her. 'Suits me,' he said. He paused. 'Let's go to the pub we went to on our first day.'

Melody couldn't help being aware of the possessive pronoun. *Our* first day suggested something familiar and intimate, something to be continued—and although at one time it would have put her on the defensive, for some reason it didn't. Because she had to admit to being totally at ease with Adam—an ease mixed with a definite feeling that she was once more on home ground. That she was actually *at* home.

How weird was that? she thought. She hadn't even taken possession of her cottage yet—not really. It was still an empty shell. But she had already made plans for the decorators to begin work next month, and soon after that the rooms would be furnished and she could begin to start thinking of her future—and how much of it would be spent there.

At the pub, the same corner table was empty, and Adam grinned at her as they sat down. 'I think this is how it all started,' he murmured.

They both decided on the seared sea bass and salad for their meal, and Melody realised just how hungry she'd been as she put down her knife and fork.

'That was fantastic,' she said. 'Though probably not to be compared with the exotic stuff you've been eating recently. How was Malaysia, by the way?'

His eyes glinted across at her. 'Still there,' he replied, 'and just as lovely.'

But not as lovely as you, Mrs Forester, he could have added, admitting to himself for the first time that he was head over heels in love with this woman. He had not stopped thinking about her since that evening in her flat. And, worryingly, what he'd interpreted then as lust was now something far, far deeper. More reliable, more lasting. But could it be trusted? Could this new gut feeling of his be trusted? And what chance did he have with her, in any case? She'd hardly thrown herself at him, he thought wryly.

He realised that he was going to have to use all his powers of persuasion to make any headway with her. But now that he'd come to terms with his own feelings—now that he'd accepted the inevitable—there was no going back. In spite of all that had happened in the past, he was going to marry Mel. However long it took.

Suddenly she sensed that something was going on in his head, and she stood up quickly, feeling uneasy. She needed to get away, to be by herself, she thought. 'I'd like to go now, Adam,' she said. 'I do feel a bit tired after the journey.'

Before he could go over to the bar she'd edged past him neatly, settling their bill with the landlord, and as she rejoined him he looked down at her. 'Thank you very much for my supper,' he said solemnly, thinking, That's the last time you'll do that for me, Mel Forester. From now on *I'm* the captain of the ship!

It was getting late as he parked the car at Poplars, but the lights were still on in the kitchen. Adam glanced in at the lighted windows as they approached the building.

'Ah, good. My parents are still up,' he said. He paused. 'Come in for a minute, Mel. I'd like you to meet them.'

Melody caught her breath for a moment as she followed Adam. His mother, Isabel, would have known Frances very well…

'Mother—Dad—' Adam began. 'I'd like to introduce you to Mel…'

'Mel…? *Melody!* It *is* Melody, isn't it? It *must* be! My dear little girl, I would know you anywhere! You are the image of your mother!' Isabel Carlisle went straight over and caught hold of Melody's hand. 'But the last time I saw you, you were just a week old! I never expected to see you ever again! What a lovely anniversary present!' The woman held Melody away from her, looking at her searchingly as a shy smile crossed the girl's face and she nodded her head in amazement. 'Robert— isn't she *exactly* like Frances?'

Robert Carlisle looked across and smiled genially. 'Yes—a beautiful replica,' he agreed.

For a few seconds after that there was complete silence, during which Adam's face was a picture of puzzlement. He looked at his mother, utterly confused.

'What's going on?' he demanded. 'And Mel is short for *Melody*? You're not Melanie, then, as we all supposed?'

'No. Melody is an unusual name,' she said, 'so I always introduce myself as Mel—which is simpler for most people to accept.'

Isabel brought her over to sit beside her. 'And… Frances…?' she began.

'My mother died six years ago,' Melody said quietly.

'Well, I'm sorry to hear that.' She paused. 'Now, tell me all about yourself, my dear.'

'Yes—*do*,' Adam said tartly, wondering how on earth his mother had any idea who Mel was.

The girl looked up at him, her face flushed. 'My mother— Frances—was housekeeper here for many years,' she began. 'You probably knew her yourself, in your early childhood.'

'And a marvellous one she was, too,' Isabel said.

'Gatehouse Cottage was where she lived all that time,' Melody went on, realising that there was no point any more in keeping up the pretence. 'And it was where I was born,' she added quietly.

Adam's face was dark, his expansive brow creased in confused annoyance. 'Were you indeed?' he said flatly. 'So why the big mystery? Why have you never mentioned any of this before?' he demanded.

Melody found difficulty in answering him. How could she tell him that she wasn't keeping her own secret, but a secret that belonged solely to her mother. It must seem very deceitful to Adam, she realised, that in the considerable time they'd spent together she'd deliberately kept him in the dark. 'It was…difficult…' was all she said.

'Why difficult? *What* was difficult? Nothing to be ashamed of, surely? I don't get it,' he said harshly.

'I…just…don't know…' Melody began miserably, wishing with all her heart that she *had* told him before this. She turned to Isabel. 'Although my mother frequently spoke of the village—of the people, and Poplars, and the cottage—she was adamant that she would never set foot here again. And she would never tell me why.' She paused, and Isabel took her hand, holding it gently in hers.

'I think I can explain—if you want me to,' she said.

Melody nodded. 'Please…' she whispered. 'I must know…' She didn't look at Adam, conscious that her heart was thumping uncomfortably. What was she going to hear?

'Thirty years ago,' Isabel said, 'the Forsythe family owned the Manor—the place across the valley from here—as well as most of the village and outlying area. It was a tremendously wealthy dynasty. The Lord of the Manor at the time was Barnaby Forsythe, who inherited it rather early in his life—still in his twenties, in fact—but rose to the task magnificently. He and his young wife Elizabeth were wonderful—popular with the whole community, and so generous to poorer families who might have sometimes found it difficult to pay the very reasonable rents on their cottages.' She paused. 'Of course times have moved on, and most of those properties are privately owned now.'

She seemed lost in thought for a moment, before continuing. 'Then, one day, a terrible tragedy occurred. Two years into their marriage Elizabeth was thrown from her horse, and overnight she became paraplegic. It was a horrible thing… They were such a glamorous couple, so much in love. Life for them, in its fullest sense, was over.' She took a tissue from her bag. 'Of course money was never a problem, and Barnaby saw that she met the top specialists, had the best of care—but what solace is money in a situation like that? I know that they would have given away every last penny just to be able to live a normal life.' She wiped a tear away from her cheek. 'We'd always been firm friends of the family, and we mourned with them. As the whole village did.'

Melody swallowed a lump in her own throat as the story unfolded. But what was this to do with *her*?

'Elizabeth and your mother knew each other, of course, and were of a similar age,' Isabel went on. 'Some years after the tragedy Elizabeth was taught to paint, holding the brush between her teeth, and Frances used to sit and paint with her for hours and hours on end. They became very close, naturally.' She glanced at Melody. 'Your mother was very artistic—an accomplished artist, wasn't she, Melody?'

Melody's mouth had begun to dry as all these facts became known, her brain desperately trying to see where she fitted in to all this.

'One summer evening, after one of their normal sessions, Elizabeth insisted that Barnaby should escort Frances back home across the fields. They'd gone on rather later than usual, it was a particularly dark night, and…'

'And Barnaby made love to Frances,' Adam said shrewdly. 'At Gatehouse Cottage.'

'Yes. He did,' Isabel said, without a trace of embarrassment. 'And the few of us who ever knew about it had every sympathy. For fifteen years—fifteen youthful years—Barnaby had lived a celibate life, tending and supporting the wife he loved with such dedication and loyalty. He was an inspiration. And on that one evening he fell into a few hours of passion with a woman he admired, respected and loved—your mother, Melody.' She held Melody's hand again. 'Frances and I were always honest with each other,' she said, 'and I believed her implicitly when she told me that she and Barnaby had been lovers for just one night and that one night only. Could anyone with a heart find fault with that?'

No one spoke for a few moments as Isabel's words began to sink in. Then the woman met Melody's gaze unfalteringly.

'I believe—I sincerely believe,' she said quietly, 'that a man is capable of loving two women equally—in exceptional circumstances, as these most certainly were. But…' She smiled briefly. 'In our culture, only one wife is allowed at one time. You were conceived in love, Melody. Never have any doubt about that. And that liaison was enough to bring into the world the only child either of them would ever have.' She paused. 'I take it that Frances never had other children?'

Melody shook her head. 'Sadly—no,' she replied quietly.

'Well, you were a true love-child, Melody,' Isabel said. She sighed. 'In the same month that Barnaby and Frances were lovers, Barnaby took Elizabeth to Australia. They stayed for a year with a branch of the family over there.' She shook her head. 'The really sad part is that it could not have had a happier ending for the three of them.'

Melody found herself floating in a sea of disbelief—and sympathetic dismay at her mother's predicament—while Adam had been stunned into silence at everything he'd heard.

'Is there more?' he asked flatly.

'Well, Frances wanted it kept secret…only a small handful of us ever knew the truth. Don't believe it when it's said that people can't be trusted to keep their mouths shut,' she added. 'Her secret was safe with us.' She paused. 'A week after your birth, Melody, you and your mother moved away, and were literally never seen here again. Until tonight, of course, when I thought you were a vision as you walked in.' She smiled.

Melody swallowed, trying hard to come to terms with all that Isabel had told her. 'And did my…father…' her *father*—she was anonymous no more! '…did my father know about me?' she asked simply.

'Not until a year later, when I took it upon myself to tell him,' Isabel replied. 'I felt it right that he should know he had a child. They were still abroad when I spoke to him about it.'

'And what was his reaction?' Adam asked, by this time as transfixed as Melody.

'He was overwhelmed. With joy,' Isabel said. 'I don't suppose he ever told Elizabeth, because her well-being was his sole concern, and he'd never have wanted to hurt her. But do you know…?' She paused for a moment. 'I believe that Elizabeth might have had a deeper reason for insisting that Barnaby should escort Frances home that night…might have hoped that what happened, would happen.' She looked up at the others. 'It's our right, as human beings, to be as one,' she said quietly, 'and I'm sure that Elizabeth felt that, too. And that she should offer—and sanction—the one precious gift she was incapable of giving.'

Robert got up from his chair. 'Yes, it was a very sad story,' he said. 'Made more so by the fact that five years later they were both killed in a road accident out there in Australia where they eventually moved after selling the Manor to the de Wintons.'

'Added to which, of course, he never ever saw his

daughter—of whom he would have been immensely proud,' Isabel said, smiling at Melody. 'Because Frances was determined not to bring the Forsythe family's name—a well-respected name in the locality—into disrepute. Their reputation should never be sullied by *her*. He tried valiantly, through me, to send maintenance for his child, but Frances was stubborn and refused. She'd gone away for good—severed all links with the village—and wanted no handouts from anyone. But in the end she reluctantly agreed to invest a very generous one-off sum for their daughter—to be given to you, Melody, on your mother's death.' She paused. '*She* wanted none of it. I tried to keep in touch with Frances, and did so for many years, but gradually we began to lose touch.' She shrugged. 'Time passes. People move on,' she said quietly.

Dazed by all this revelation, Melody felt her senses swimming. No wonder she felt so much part of the place, she thought. She was a daughter of this soil! She had come back to her roots…in every sense. And of *course*! In a blinding flash she realised where her legacy had really come from! Not from her aunt at all—of course not! There'd been no money there to speak of. That gift was her father's gift…a gift which had enabled her to buy Gatehouse Cottage. And which had brought her life full-circle!

## CHAPTER THIRTEEN

SLOWLY, Melody got up from her chair, wondering whether she had the strength to go up the stairs to her room. She was both exhilarated and exhausted by the unbelievable news she'd just been given. Looking quickly at Adam, she was rewarded with a stony-faced expression that sent her heart plummeting. He was annoyed—of course he was! And she had some explaining to do!

The older couple stood up, too. 'I think it's time for bed,' Isabel said. 'It'll be a long day tomorrow—and then on Sunday we're having a celebration lunch here at Poplars, Melody. We've arranged for people in the village to do the catering, because we don't want Fee to have anything else to do at the moment—we do hope you'll join us for that.' She smiled. 'In fact, it will make our day to have Frances and Barnaby's daughter to share it with us.' She dropped a light kiss on Melody's cheek, then hugged Adam before going towards the door. 'Goodnight, my dears—and sleep well.'

After they'd gone, Melody faced Adam, trying not to look as guilty as she felt. He stared back at her.

'Well, what a complete fool you've made of me,' he said harshly, and his meltingly sexy tones suddenly held a distinct air of menace. 'You must have been having a good laugh at my expense.' He snorted derisively. 'I do hope you've enjoyed the joke!' He paused. 'But what a curious game you've been playing, Mrs Forester.'

'I haven't been playing a game,' Melody replied quietly, trying to stop herself from trembling. She had just been given the most amazing news about herself, about her own life, and she was finding it difficult to take it in all at once. But now she had to try and appease Adam—he did, after all, deserve some sort of apology.

'Well, what do *you* call it, then? Am I allowed an explanation?' He almost spat out the words.

'Please, Adam. I'll do my best to get you to understand.'

He shoved a chair to one side and sat down, leaning back and looking at her coldly. 'Go on, then,' he said. 'Why the big mystery? What on earth was *that* all about?'

Melody didn't sit, but stayed where she was, one hand gripping the side of the table for support. 'It wasn't something I felt I could talk about—to anyone,' she said. 'Because I had no idea why my mother had refused to come back here—though it's much clearer now! There was obviously a secret, but she would never talk to me about it, maintaining that the past should be the past.'

'Not dwelling on the past is one thing,' Adam said shortly. 'Ignoring it, pretending it hasn't happened, is another. Far better to confront it, deal with it—and move on.'

'And that is exactly what I think I was trying to do,' Melody said quietly. 'Enough time had passed since my mother's death for me to feel that I should come here and just…well, just *be*… Though I had no real expectation that I would discover anything.'

'But all the times we've been together—especially at the cottage—and you never volunteered a single thing!' Adam said. 'And being so secretive about your connection here—I mean, you *knew* you'd been born here, at least! It smacks of dishonesty, deceit, Mel.' He ran a hand through his hair. 'I feel as if I've been taken for a very long ride!'

Melody was stung to respond to that. She'd never been accused of dishonesty before!

'Dishonesty by omission, perhaps,' she retorted. 'But let's not forget what we're actually talking about here, Adam. We're talking about *my* life, *my* past, *my* history! Surely what I wish to reveal is *my* business?' She paused, conscious that her knees were shaking. 'What I felt I had to do was keep faith with my mother's wishes, and I still don't know if she'd be pleased that I've come here or not. But I am so relieved to know, at last, what I was not allowed to know before. And after hearing the truth— after hearing all that your parents told me—I *understand*. For the first time I can understand…and…strangely…I can start to feel—well, complete.'

Neither of them spoke for a moment, then Adam said, 'Well, I congratulate you on being able to keep things close to your chest! It must take practice to be that devious. I mean, how have you managed to keep it up? How have you managed not to let one tiny word slip that might have told us where you were born, who you really were….'

'Because I didn't *know* who I was!' Melody shot back. 'I knew I'd been born here. That was all. In coming here on holiday I had the vaguest hope that something might explain my mother's determination to stay away for ever.'

Melody sat down now, filled with such a strange mixture of emotions she didn't know whether to laugh or cry. But her overwhelming sense was one of gratitude—gratitude for her mother's obvious integrity, and gratitude at knowing, at last, who her father was. She had to admit to an intense feeling of pride in belonging to Barnaby Forsythe, in sharing the blood-line of a man who had loved so deeply—not just the woman he'd married, and to whom he'd been devoted, but also the woman he'd come to love as well: her mother. *Whatever* Adam Carlisle said, families were the ultimate tie—the ultimate strength of human bonding, she thought. To be loyal, to love and be loved—there was nothing more important in the whole world. What else did anyone need?

The unusual, uncomfortable silence between them told Melody that Adam was not won over by her explanation of her position in all this. He stood up.

'Well, I think that one day you should try your luck in politics,' he said unkindly. 'The only qualification you need is to be a convincing actress—and you're certainly that, Mel. Acting mixed with a little cunning might even get you the position of prime minister!'

Melody gave him a long, measured look, her lips set. 'Your opinion is of very little interest to me,' she said coldly. 'My conscience is clear—even if you don't see it that way. All I can do is apologise that I didn't feel able to tell you what you now know about me. I've explained my reasons.' She picked up her bag. 'Goodnight, Adam.'

She went to go past him, but he thrust himself up from the chair, pulling her to him, pinning her arms to her sides—and then his mouth came down on to hers in an angry movement. She felt his tongue probing her lips and she gasped—in surprise and shock at the suddenness of what he was doing. Then in a moment of unbelievable surrender she collapsed into his arms. This evening's revelations had been too much for her to cope with—she needed support, and she wanted someone to rejoice with, she thought desperately. She needed Adam!

Almost at once the ferocity of his kiss changed into the sort of breathtaking passion that she'd missed so much over the last year, and she clung to him. For a few timeless moments they stayed locked together, each lost in their own thoughts, each wallowing in their sudden intimacy, until Melody pulled right away, looking up at him, her eyes glowing with desire—and disillusionment!

Hadn't he just called her deceitful—and *cunning*? Horrible, hurtful words! But her problem was, she realised, that he did have a point. To him she must seem unnecessarily secretive— yet if she'd told him that she'd been born in Gatehouse Cottage what a can of worms that would have opened! Questions would have followed—most of which, until half an hour ago, she'd had no answer to. But he'd never understand, she thought. He was not in the frame of mind to even try.

After a moment she turned away and left the room without another word.

He just stood there, motionless, listening to her light footsteps tread softly up the stairs. Then he pushed his chair back, scraping it harshly on the tiled floor. He still felt totally staggered at what he'd heard about Melody's past—how she had transmuted from casual tourist to direct descendent of the Forsythe clan! She'd turned up here from nowhere when, amazingly, Gatehouse Cottage had been up for auction, and she, a complete stranger, had won it. But of course she was no stranger after all. He thrust his hands in his pockets. To think that if fate had handled things differently she might have ended up as Lady of the Manor in her own right! A slow smile spread briefly across his handsome features. Fate could be an unpredictable mistress!

It was nearly one o'clock in the morning, and he remembered that he'd promised Callum to do the last rounds tonight, before turning in himself. So, with the dogs safely asleep in front of the Aga, he switched off the lights and left the room, locking the heavy front door securely, before making his way noise-lessly through the building. It was quiet everywhere, but he stood outside Mel's room for a few moments, listening, remem-bering all too clearly that other night when she'd been so upset.

Presently, back in his own room, he sat on the edge of his bed for a moment. A couple of months ago he'd known nothing of this woman's existence—but he knew about it now! And he admitted to himself again that he had fallen for her—completely. Nothing could change that now. Come what may, Melody Forester was going to be Mrs Adam Carlisle—whatever the cost! But would he ever really be able to trust her? Oh, he didn't mean in the accepted sense—he was certain that she was not the sort to play around with other men—but her ability to keep so quiet about herself over all these weeks had to say something about her, surely? If she could deceive on that level what else was she capable of? And if he couldn't trust her, what chance would a serious relationship have?

He gritted his teeth—he'd risk it! He'd somehow make this come right. Despite all his preconceptions about marriage, he'd put his head in the noose once again—and risk being throttled! he thought. Because, quite simply, he couldn't help himself. She had bewitched him totally, and he wanted to spend the rest of his life with her. Loving her, protecting her, sharing himself with her. All he had to do now was convince her to see his point of view…

The next morning Melody arrived down for breakfast rather late—all the other paying guests had already gone. But Isabel and Robert were there, drinking their coffee, and they looked up as she came in, greeting her warmly.

She helped herself to rolls and fruit juice, but declined a cooked meal from the girl who was serving breakfasts that morning.

'Another wonderfully warm day,' Robert observed, smiling over at Melody.

'Oh, they always manage to have it just right for this event,' Isabel said cheerfully. 'And practically everyone gets involved…it's a real community affair. Adam always tries to get home in time for it—likes making himself useful in whatever way he can,' she added fondly. 'He usually gets roped in to take his turn in the stocks, for the children to throw wet sponges at him!'

Melody smiled inwardly. After all the names he'd called her last night, she'd queue up to hurl a few, she thought.

There was silence for a few moments, then Isabel said, 'Melody, I do hope that everything I told you—you know, about your mother—didn't upset you too much, my dear. We did think afterwards that it would have come as something of a shock, perhaps…'

Melody smiled. 'I wasn't upset,' she said carefully. Well, not about that, anyway, she thought. 'I'm grateful to you for telling me. Not that it will make any significant difference to my life in a practical sense, but speaking emotionally it has made all the difference in the world. I feel a…whole person, now, rather than half a one.' She hesitated. 'It would have been so good to have had a sister—or a brother.'

'Well, it certainly *can* be…' Isabel began, glancing at her husband, who was pouring himself more coffee. 'But sadly for us our two—Adam and Rupert, our twins—have never got on. It's such a shame.'

Melody caught her breath. Was she going to be told what she wanted to know? She threw discretion to the winds. 'Why?' she asked softly. 'What went wrong?'

'It was not Adam's fault,' Robert cut in. 'I'm afraid Rupert has a very jealous streak—sorry though we are to say it—and try as we did, we can do nothing about it.' He paused. 'Regrettable though it is, people are as they are, and that's all there is to it. The boys were never treated any differently—we love them both equally. But it's always seemed to be Adam who finds it so easy to succeed in everything—academically, in sports—and he was always very popular with women, who seem drawn to him like bees to a honey pot. Whereas Rupert has always found that side of things very difficult. Always had a chip on his shoulder about something or other. Silly chap. His own worst enemy.' He drank from his cup. 'But we have to hand it to Adam—he always tried valiantly to pour oil on troubled waters, because he knew how upset we were, as he was himself.' He paused. 'But now our boys have not spoken for two whole years.'

The emptiness in their hearts was palpable as Melody listened.

Isabel went on, 'Then, of course, the unbelievable—the worst thing of all happened—'

Robert cut in. 'Oh, don't spoil the day by bringing all that up, Isabel,' he said. 'Keep it for another time. This is our celebration weekend, remember!'

They all stood up, then, to leave, and Melody said quietly, 'Maybe it will all come right one day?' she suggested. 'Old sores can sometimes heal…'

Isabel sighed. 'I'd love to think so, Melody. But the damage is done, I'm afraid. And there's no undoing it.'

So, Melody thought, as they went their separate ways, Adam had a secret of his own! Whatever could it be?

Later, wearing a cream cotton sundress, Melody made her way up to the field and the village hall. Even before she got there she could hear music, raised voices and laughter. The place was packed with people enjoying all the sideshows, and children darted around excitedly. She decided to go straight to the hall, where she knew Fee would be.

'Hi, Mel,' Fee said, as she came up. 'See—your fruit has been snapped up!'

'Well, I hope there's something left for me to buy—' Melody began, but Fee cut in.

'There's certainly no need for you to buy fruit! We've packed the rest of it, all ready for you to take back with you.' She glanced up briefly. 'Adam's up at the other end of the field, doing sterling duty at the carousel—which, would you believe, has packed up. Something to do with the generator. He's offered to work the thing by hand so as not to disappoint the children.

Good job it's confined to the under-sevens,' she added, 'or he'd be doing himself a mischief!'

Melody was surprised. She hadn't thought Adam was a child-lover—not enough to put himself out, anyway. But later on, as she made her way along the field, she could see the gaudy carousel moving rapidly around—and Adam standing in the centre, his hands stretched above his head as he grasped and pushed the metal rods so that the six little cars could circulate to the obvious delight of the small occupants. He was so engrossed in the task that he didn't see her for several minutes. But suddenly their eyes met, and despite all the heated feelings of last night, they both smiled at each other.

Melody's heart missed a beat. He was so unutterably gorgeous, she thought, his suntanned skin shining with perspiration, his hair glistening blackly in the hot sunshine. And when he smiled at her like that she felt a rush of such passionate excitement that she felt ashamed at the longing in her heart. What had this man done to her? Had he completely robbed her of her common sense?

'If you're waiting for a turn,' he called over affably, 'I'm afraid you don't qualify.'

'Then there's no point in waiting in the queue,' she called back with a smile in her voice, thinking that the collective weight of those tinies must be considerable.

Presently, after she'd spent some money on the various stalls, and bought several raffle tickets, Melody made her way back to the hall, where she and Fee were going to have lunch together. Fee was already there, sitting at a table, and Melody went across to join her.

'Everything's going well out there,' Melody said, sitting down. 'All the tins are rattling with money!'

'You're not bored, are you, Mel?' Fee said. 'I mean, this isn't really your sort of thing, is it?'

'I'm not bored at all!' Melody said. 'I love the atmosphere. Everyone's so friendly.'

There was a lull in the conversation, then Fee said, 'I want you to know that Isabel told us—Callum and me—everything she told you last night, Mel. And it came as a rather wonderful surprise,' she added. 'We none of us had any idea that Barnaby Forsythe had fathered a child. Of course we were only children ourselves at the time. It's an amazing story, isn't it? And amazing that you should turn up, after all this time, and buy Gatehouse Cottage.'

'I wonder if I shall ever feel *unamazed* ever again!'

Fee touched Melody's hand briefly. 'We shall love knowing you're down at the cottage,' she said earnestly. 'Even if it isn't very often.'

'I shall make it as often as I possibly can!' Melody exclaimed.

Much later, after she'd watched the races, and the tug-of-war—where, naturally, Adam and Callum were on the winning side—Melody wandered back to Poplars. The Carlisles had insisted on booking a table for the six of them at the Rose & Crown for supper, but now Melody decided that she wanted to be by herself for a while. To come to terms with her new identity. Even though she knew it would not make a scrap of difference to her future life, it entirely changed her perception of her past. She decided that she'd go for that lovely walk across the fields, where she'd picked the flowers.

It was a beautiful early autumn evening, the sun still warm as she trod the now familiar route. Her personal jigsaw was complete, she thought—so why wasn't she feeling as euphoric as she should be?

Twenty minutes later she came to the field which led to the stream she'd bathed her feet in—which subsequent rainfall had added to considerably. The water now gurgled and chuckled along, and Melody dropped to her knees, scooping up a handful to put to her lips. She didn't know whether she was doing a wise thing or not, but it tasted wonderfully sweet on her tongue as she took another generous gulp. Adam's voice interrupted.

'What a charming picture,' he said.

Melody leaned back on her heels and looked up. He crouched down beside her, so that their faces were close, his white teeth glistening as he gave her that slow, incredible smile.

'Can you ever forgive me?' he said softly. 'After all the things I said last night?'

'Adam,' Melody said, 'when I really thought about it afterwards, I realised how deeply hurt you must have felt at my…deviousness…'

He put a finger on her lips gently. 'Please, Mel—please don't go on,' he said. 'What you actually proved, and what I didn't see then, was your total loyalty. That you would always keep your word. I had no right to speak as I did. But…but I thought I might lose you.'

'Lose me?'

'I was afraid that I would lose my trust in you…that you might be capable of…' He was finding it difficult to find the right words. 'Of betraying me,' he added.

'But how would I do that?' Melody frowned.

'I was afraid that in future I might not always feel absolutely sure of you, Mel…'

Melody shook her head slowly. 'You've lost me, Adam.'

He took both her hands in his. 'I want you, Mel. I want you to marry me. I want us to be together for all time, with no secrets between us—ever.'

Melody refrained from gasping out loud at this unexpected proposal of marriage—and at the heat that rushed right through the length of her body at his words.

She returned his penetrating gaze with her own steady, patently honest green eyes. She knew that his own troubled past was somehow etched into his words, and she said, 'First can I be allowed to learn your own secret, Adam? About Rupert? Your parents were explaining that your brother can be difficult…'

Still holding her hands tightly, he said, 'I was once engaged to be married. To Lucy. The wedding was planned, arrangements made—and I thought she was the one for me. Then one day Rupert made the surprise announcement that he'd had a fling with my intended wife, and that she was expecting his baby.'

Melody was horrified. No wonder Adam was cynical about relationships!

'It was bad enough for me,' he went on, 'but in a way worse for my parents, who felt that Rupert had betrayed us all. Betrayed the whole family.' He shrugged. 'As it happened, Lucy lost the baby early on, and their affair ground to a halt. He was never serious about her,' he added grimly. 'My brother only wanted to prove that he could get one over me. Take what was mine.' He took a deep breath. 'We haven't spoken since. So…' He paused. 'That's my secret, Mel. And that's all there is.'

Melody looked at him with such an overpowering need to hold him in her arms that she whispered softly, 'Make love to me, Adam.'

He gazed down at her for a long, tense moment, and then without another word he put his arms around her and lowered her to the ground slowly. Carefully he undressed her, touching her half-closed eyes, the tip of her nose, the smooth skin at the base of her neck and then her firm, aching breasts with his mouth and tongue, heightening her unashamed passion to such an excited level that she thought she was going to cry out.

'I love you, Mel,' he said softly. 'And I want you.'

Then, effortlessly, he undressed himself and knelt up, raising himself above her. And under the mellowing sky, with nature all around them, they made unhurried, tender, sensuous love—until, exhausted, they lay back on the soft turf.

After a few silent moments, Adam turned his head to look at her. 'You'll have to marry me now,' he murmured.

Suddenly the impact of his words stabbed at her painfully. Hadn't she vowed never to truly love again? Hadn't she vowed never again to risk loss and the emptiness of being alone? But how could she resist Adam's powerful masculinity? How could she resist the thought of lying in his arms night after night for the rest of her life?

Without looking at him, she said, 'So—what would happen? Where would we live?'

He waited before answering. 'At the Manor, of course,' he replied. 'Your rightful home. The de Wintons have sold it to me—we've been in negotiations all the summer.'

'But what about Malaysia?' she asked.

'Oh, did I forget to say? We're selling up—selling the business. My parents are well into their seventies. I shall have my share of the proceeds, to make what I will of my life. I knew I'd always intended coming back here eventually, and the Manor coming up for sale seemed too good a chance to miss.' He looked down at her. 'And what more appropriate wife could I possibly ask for?'

A thousand thoughts invaded Melody's brain—tormenting her, warning her.

'I want to say yes, Adam, I really do,' she whispered. 'But I'm *afraid*.'

'Afraid? What of? Not of me, surely?' he said, bringing her close to him.

'No. I'm afraid of losing again—afraid of losing you,' she said simply. 'I'm afraid to trust fate, that's all.'

He understood what she was saying. 'Don't you think we're in the same boat?' he said gently. 'I'm afraid of betrayal; you're afraid of loss. But that's not the way to live a life, and you know it, Mel. We *have* to trust—trust our love, trust each other.' His mouth came down onto hers again. 'We have to trust in *hope*. And keep our fingers crossed,' he added, smiling faintly.

Around the long table in the kitchen of Poplars the next day, the atmosphere was electrically charged—to such an extent that, not for the first time, Melody thought she was going to burst with excitement and anticipation. The Golden Wedding Anniversary had been given due attention and congratulation— but it was Melody and Adam who were now the centre of the celebrations.

Fee and Callum were all smiles, and Adam's parents were ecstatic.

'We were afraid that Adam would never find anyone else,' Isabel confided to Melody, as yet more wine was being passed around. 'We are both so happy about it, Melody. It just seems so…*right*, somehow.'

Melody hugged her affectionately. 'On the scale of happiness,' she said simply, 'my own is off the top!'

The main meal—deliciously presented by the caterers— had come to an end, and presently Fee said, 'Now there's just one more thing to be sorted…shan't be a sec.'

Adam, sitting close to Melody, his hand holding hers tightly, said quietly, 'We mustn't forget the dogs. They deserve a walk after all the noise we've been making.'

'Let's go, then,' she whispered. 'I need some fresh air!'

Then the door opened, and Fee came in bearing an iced celebration cake, alive with lighted candles—followed by a rather spare man with tousled brown hair.

There was a moment's stunned silence, then Isabel rose quickly to her feet.

'*Rupert!*' she exclaimed. 'My dear Rupert—we didn't think for a moment that…'

Callum got up. 'This is all down to my wife,' he explained,

shooting a quick glance at Adam. 'She thought it was right to remind Rupert what a special weekend this was for you, Mr and Mrs Carlisle. So we got in touch, and—and, well, here he is.'

The next few moments passed in a haze for Melody, as Isabel and Robert embraced Rupert—whom she could see did not much resemble his brother in any way. He looked tired and unsure of himself—unsure of the reception he'd get, at least from Adam.

Adam went over and held out his hand. 'Hi, bro,' he said quietly. 'Long time, no see.'

The two men shook hands, and for a moment nothing was said by anyone. But Isabel was crying silently, and Robert suddenly needed a handkerchief to blow his nose loudly.

'I need to say something,' Rupert said, his voice a little unsteady. 'I've needed to say it for some time, but I've only just found the courage.' He hesitated. 'I've come to wish my parents another fifty happy years together—but most of all I've come to ask your forgiveness. All of you. But especially you, Adam.' He turned away, gathering his courage to go on. 'I've thought of this moment so many times in the last two years—wondered whether you'd ever speak to me again. But I hope you will. Because I've missed you. I've missed all of you. I've had a rotten couple of years since I left the firm—since I ruined your plans, Adam. I thought I could do much better by myself—doing my own thing, no ties, no shackles, that kind of thing. I was wrong. I need you. I need all of you. But will you ever want me, ever again?'

Without a word Adam put his arms around his brother's neck and held him tightly. 'Don't go on, Rupert,' he said huskily. 'Because I want to thank you—from the bottom of my heart.'

'Thank me?'

Adam turned and held out his hand to Melody, who came across at once. 'Meet the girl of my dreams,' he said softly. 'This is Melody, who is going to be my wife. And if you hadn't taken Lucy off my hands—well, I wouldn't be free, would I? You saved me for another day, Rupert—and it will be the best day of my whole life.'

Four months later Adam and Melody sat either side of Fee's hospital bed, with Melody cradling Master Toby Adam Brown in her arms.

'Now we know how it's done,' Callum joked, 'this is only the beginning! We've warned the entire village to expect an influx of small Brown kids, running wild about the place.'

'I still can't really believe it,' Fee said, looking wan but deliriously happy. 'Our luck seems to have changed with your arrival, Melody.' She glanced at Adam. 'Everything seems to have come right. For all of us.'

'Amen to that,' Adam said. 'But I suppose your work on Gatehouse Cottage will have to wait for a while now, Callum?'

'Oh, it'll all happen—in its own time,' Callum said good-naturedly. 'We've got our baby, we've got the cottage, and we've got the rest of our lives. We don't need another thing.'

Fee took the baby from Melody and looked up at her. 'Thank you for postponing the wedding so that I can be behind you on the day, Mel,' she said. 'I've never been bridesmaid to anyone before. I can't wait!'

'*You* can't wait!' Adam exclaimed, putting his arm firmly around Melody's waist. 'How d'you think *I'm* feeling?'

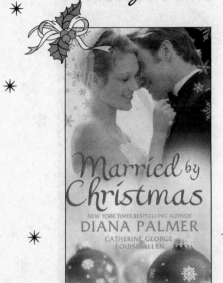

# *Celebrate 100 years of pure reading pleasure with Mills & Boon®*

To mark our centenary, each month we're publishing a special 100th Birthday Edition. These celebratory editions are packed with extra features and include a FREE bonus story.

Plus, you have the chance to enter a fabulous monthly prize draw. See 100th Birthday Edition books for details.

*Now that's worth celebrating!*

### September 2008

**Crazy about her Spanish Boss by Rebecca Winters**
Includes FREE bonus story
*Rafael's Convenient Proposal*

### November 2008

**The Rancher's Christmas Baby
by Cathy Gillen Thacker**
Includes FREE bonus story *Baby's First Christmas*

### December 2008

**One Magical Christmas by Carol Marinelli**
Includes FREE bonus story *Emergency at Bayside*

Look for Mills & Boon® 100th Birthday Editions at your favourite bookseller or visit
www.millsandboon.co.uk

# FREE

## 4 BOOKS AND A SURPRISE GIFT!

We would like to take this opportunity to thank you for reading this Mills & Boon® book by offering you the chance to take FOUR more specially selected titles from the Modern™ series absolutely FREE! We're also making this offer to introduce you to the benefits of the Mills & Boon® Book Club—

★ **FREE home delivery**
★ **FREE gifts and competitions**
★ **FREE monthly Newsletter**
★ **Books available before they're in the shops**
★ **Exclusive Mills & Boon® Book Club offers**

Accepting these FREE books and gift places you under no obligation to buy; you may cancel at any time, even after receiving your free shipment. Simply complete your details below and return the entire page to the address below. You don't even need a stamp!

**YES!** Please send me 4 free Modern books and a surprise gift. I understand that unless you hear from me, I will receive 6 superb new titles every month for just £2.99 each, postage and packing free. I am under no obligation to purchase any books and may cancel my subscription at any time. The free books and gift will be mine to keep in any case.

P8ZEE

Ms/Mrs/Miss/Mr..............................Initials ...........................
BLOCK CAPITALS PLEASE

Surname ...........................................................................................

Address ...........................................................................................

...........................................................................................

..............................................Postcode ...........................

Send this whole page to:
The Mills & Boon Book Club, FREEPOST CN81, Croydon, CR9 3WZ